ز

TERRELL L. BOWERS

GARRETT'S
TRAIL TO
JUSTICE

Complete and Unabridged

LINFORD
Leicester

First published in Great Britain in 2014 by
Robert Hale Limited
London

First Linford Edition
published 2016
by arrangement with
Robert Hale
an imprint of The Crowood Press
Wiltshire

A catalogue record for this book is available
from the British Library.

ISBN 978–1–4448–3039–2

Published by
F. A. Thorpe (Publishing)
Anstey, Leicestershire

Set by Words & Graphics Ltd.
Anstey, Leicestershire
Printed and bound in Great Britain by
T. J. International Ltd., Padstow, Cornwall

This book is printed on acid-free paper

GARRETT'S TRAIL
TO JUSTICE

Dayton Garrett is a roving trouble-shooter, taking on jobs from town-taming to bringing down a counterfeiting ring. Charged with searching for a missing child, he fetches up in Shilo, where his attorney brother Knute provides him with helpful information — and requests a favour in return. Alyson Walsh has been convicted of murder in a kangaroo court, and faces the noose in two days' time. Knute wants her broken out of jail while he endeavours to get her a fair trial — and Dayton is just the man for the job . . .

1

'Grab anything you can,' Alyson's mother pleaded softly, her voice barely audible. 'Don't come back without something for us to eat.' The woman reached out a feeble hand and gently stroked Alyson's face. 'I know 'tis a mighty burden, dear daughter, but we have nothing left.'

Alyson nodded her head obediently, though she loathed the idea of walking the streets begging or trying to steal bread or food for the two of them. There was also a lot of competition. The Great Famine, as it was being called, had devastated the Ireland potato crop for the fifth year in a row. There were stories going around that women and children were being shipped to Australia, thousands of them. Her mother said it was a plan to try and save the remainder of those

1

still trying to survive in their home-
land. Never had a potato blight lasted
so long. A great number of people had
died from starvation and many men
deserted their families in hopes the
tenuous charity system would provide
for them. Some men of weaker
character, like her father, ran away
simply to try and save themselves.

Alyson spent the next few hours
prowling the nearby farms and houses,
seeking any morsel of food. When she
failed to find even a mere scrap, she
ventured into town and began her hunt.
It was a terrible existence with no relief
in sight. Reduced to stealing to live for
the past several weeks, Alyson had only
managed a few hard rolls, a handful of
limes and a small bag of mostly rotten
potatoes. Each time she had managed
to slip away unseen, or had outrun the
store owner. But the people had
become more vigilant, guarding what
few goods they had, and ever on the
alert for children walking alone. Some
had even hired teenage youths to

discourage theft or run down a stealer.

Before attempting outright thievery, Alyson begged at a number of shops and even tried her luck on the street. It was of little use, as she had to compete with dozens of other children, beggars of all ages, and even women with babies in their arms. So many were starving; it simply overwhelmed the few who were able to support themselves.

Alyson finally made a desperate attempt, snatching a loaf of bread from just inside a shop. But she was spotted and pursued by a teenage boy. He caught her after a short run and dragged her back to the store owner. The man ignored her crying and pleas and turned her over to the local authorities.

Locked in a room with several other thieves, Alyson's turn came for her to be taken to the local magistrate. She was led to one of the main buildings in town and escorted to a small office. She couldn't read the printing on the door, but a portly man, attired in a rather drab suit and seated behind a desk, gave her a tired and somewhat exasperated look.

'Where is your mother, child?' he asked.

'Please, sir,' Alyson gave him the most pitiful expression she could manage, 'me mum is too weak to stand up. I didn't want to steal, but we've had nothing to eat for three days.'

He had obviously heard the same story a thousand times. 'I asked you where she is.'

'At the second bridge crossing leading out to MacAuley's farm. Me father worked there until the potatoes went bad again this season. He said he would return for us, but he never came back.'

The man summoned a clerk and sent a runner to take some help and locate Alyson's mother. In the meantime she was returned to the room of confinement again. After an hour or two had passed she was again collected to visit the man behind the desk.

'I'm sorry,' the man began, once Alyson was seated on a hard wooden chair. 'It seems your mother didn't have enough life left in her to wait for your return. Her body is being moved to the cemetery.' He took out a ledger, opened it to a page and spoke gently, but with purpose.

'What was your mother's name?'

Alyson had to swallow her grief before she could squeak out, 'Tara Walsh.'

'Do you have any relatives, anyone here who can care for you?'

'No one,' Alyson replied. ''Tis why me father left. We had no place to go.'

'What is your full name and age, child?' the man asked.

'Alyson Walsh,' she replied meekly. 'Seven years old.'

A minute trace of compassion entered the man's otherwise haggard face. 'These are bad times, lassie.' He stated the obvious. 'There are no funds or food to support all of the needy people in the country. To save your life and the lives of many like you, we are dispatching passenger ships to Australia. When you arrive, someone will look out for you and make you a new home.'

'Me mother said everyone there is a criminal — killers and thieves.'

'Not so, lassie,' he riposted. 'It has grown into a new country, with a working government and mills, farms and ranches. Cities are thriving and there are many opportunities for its people.'

'You going to send me there? To Australia?'

'We can't feed or house so many orphans and starving people, Alyson,' he explained. 'There's no other place to go. We must take these drastic measures if we are to save our country.'

Tears formed tiny trails down Alyson's cheeks. Her heart ached for the loss of her mother, and she was filled with hatred for the man who had deserted them. Now she was being sent across the sea, away from the only home she had ever known. She was alone . . . completely unwanted and alone. If only . . .

*   *   *

The clang of metal striking the cell bars woke Alyson from the dreaded recurring memory. It had been so many years, and still the dream came to haunt her. She sat up on the prison cot and rubbed the sleep from her eyes. It was ridiculous that a condemned prisoner ought to have to eat so early in the morning. After all, she had nothing to do all day to occupy her time until the noon meal of bread and water.

'Here you go, beautiful.' Deputy Lynch sneered the words. 'I've brung you a royal treat for your breakfast. Hope you don't choke on the mush and stale bread.' He laughed derisively. 'It would be bad manners if you died before the noose was even around your neck.'

Alyson did not reply. She had not

spoken a word since the judge declared she would be hanged for murder. With her eyes lowered, she moved to the cell door and accepted the cup of water, crust of bread, and bowl of oatmeal. Turning about, she returned to the bed, sat down, and stirred the mush to make sure it held no surprises. Fortunately, the sheriff, even though he was the cousin of the man she had killed, was a decent sort. He forbade any tormenting or mistreatment of an inmate. To his credit, he often checked to see she had been properly treated.

Alyson paused before taking a bite to offer up a silent prayer.

'Best be praying that the rope breaks your neck, sweetheart.' Lynch had been watching. 'It takes a long time to die by strangling.'

Alyson ignored his morbid teasing. She tasted the oatmeal and was relieved to find that the preparer had added a little salt. It wasn't good, but it was edible.

'Anything you need — perfume, new

shoes, a cast-iron neck brace?' Lynch continued his mocking but still failed to elicit a response.

Weary of being ignored, Deputy Lynch finally left her alone and went back to the outer office. Alyson began to eat, not because of hunger, but because it was the only thing she could do to pass the time. Two more days until her hanging, forty-eight hours until she was paraded out in front of a curious crowd of spectators to have a rope put about her neck. *At least the dreams will end,* she consoled herself. The dreadful loneliness and misery of her daily existence would be at an end.

When finished with the pitiful excuse for a meal, she cleaned up as best she could and made up her bed. Sitting down once more, she would spend the day contemplating what might have been and beseech God that, when dropped through the gallows trapdoor, the rope would mercifully break her neck.

★ ★ ★

Shilo, California, was nestled in a little valley between several working gold-fields and a major trail to San Francisco. With adequate water and fertile soil it had grown into a thriving settlement that served travelers, gold seekers and pilgrim families from all over the country. Prosperous and booming since it was founded, the bulk of the businesses and land were controlled by the Bismark family, German immigrants who had seen a way to make a fortune from the goldfields without digging in dirt and rock or living in a tent.

As he stopped his mare and pack-mule at the crest of a hill, Dayton Garrett recalled what he knew about Shilo. From the viewpoint, he gazed down upon the many wooden struc-tures and the wide main street of the town. There were a half-dozen saloons, a city hall, school, church, taverns, inns and shops of all kinds. Shilo was more than a makeshift town, it was a miniature city. Beyond Shilo were crops of corn, wheat and produce. Also he had passed several ranches with sheep, pigs, goats and cattle. Shilo appeared to be a self-supporting little burg.

Touching his heels to his mount, Dayton picked up the well-traveled road a short way from town and entered down the main street. A short way past a saddle shop and a sheriff's office was a bakery. He spotted a sign hanging from a corner bracket and knew he'd found the right place.

After tying off his animals Dayton paused to admire his brother's shingle which read: *Knute Garrett, Attorney at Law*. Then he went up an outside stairway to reach an entrance to a second-story office. He tapped once, was rewarded by a 'Come on in!' from inside and pushed open the door. The interior was a combination of office and bedroom apartment. From its dimensions and a nicely painted partition, it appeared that the upper floor was shared with the owners of the bakery below. Knute looked up from his desk, where he had been busy writing something.

'Dee!' he cried warmly, rising up to extend his hand.

'Long time,' Dayton said, moving forward to shake his brother's hand. 'Been what . . . eight or nine years?'

'Ever since you left home and went off to win the war,' Knute replied, sitting back down and waiting until Dayton had taken a chair opposite him at his desk. Then he said, 'I was glad when you contacted me.'

'I figured you might know of a way to help me find the kid I'm looking for,' Dayton replied. 'You said you had a list for me?'

'Yes. I contacted the state offices in Sacramento,' Knute said. 'The agency handling child affairs offered to provide the list, but also wants to empower you to complete a questionnaire concerning any and all of the wards you contact. Suits your needs and the state gets something in return. It will also give you limited authority in case someone doesn't want the state looking into their affairs.'

'Shouldn't be much of a chore,' Dayton said. 'Especially with the name of the one I'm looking for on the list.'

'So you've been searching for a child of a friend of yours?'

'Yes,' Dayton replied. 'There's a little more to it than that, but finding the child is the first step.'

'Mom will be proud.' Knute praised Dayton's efforts. 'Never figured you to be such a Good Samaritan.'

'Yeah, I'm full of surprises.'

'Have you seen her yet?' Knute wanted to know.

'I hope to get down that way once this job is finished.'

Kunte turned serious. 'Uh, Dee, there is another reason I'm glad you're here. Can you spare a few minutes?'

'Sure thing, big brother. What's on your mind?'

Knute deliberated for a few moments,

as if deciding what he wanted to say. Dayton waited patiently, too long absent from the family to know how his brother's mind worked. There had never been a close bond between him and Knute. Knute was ten years older than he was and had gone off to college during Dayton's last two years at home. Dayton joined the Union to fight the Confederacy at eighteen, so his memories of Knute were distant and vague. The frequent letters between him and his mother had provided information about Knute's progress and whereabouts. Now married with a child of four or five, this was where Knute had decided to hang his shingle.

'I've been keeping tabs on you, little brother.' Knute spoke along the same line. 'I see Mom several times a year and she is always relating stories about your exciting and adventurous life.'

Dayton shrugged. 'I reckon she added a little frosting to the cake, but I've managed to stay busy.'

'Town-tamer in Colorado, involved in

a range war over in Wyoming, helped the Treasury Department bring down a counterfeit ring, and even pinned on a deputy's badge with the US Marshal office on occasion.'

'I've had a scrape or two,' Dayton admitted. 'Is that what this is about? Are you in some kind of trouble?'

'First off,' Knute removed several sheets of paper, 'here's the list I got from Sacramento. They included all of the pertinent information for every ward in this part of the country.'

Dayton looked over one page and then another. 'The boy's here!' he exclaimed happily, finding the name for which he was searching. 'This is exactly what I needed. He's at a ranch that has . . . ' he counted quickly, 'whoa! they have thirty-five wards listed.'

'Plantation workers,' Knute surmised. 'Can't buy slaves, but you can put kids to work for pennies a month.' He grunted his displeasure. 'I suppose it beats having those orphans begging on the streets.'

'It links to something I've been working on,' Dayton told his brother. 'I'll head up there and see where all of this leads.'

'Just remember, I agreed to have you verify the status of each of the names whenever you contact the people who are caring for wards of the state. The Department doesn't have the funds to do a lot of follow-ups after the placement of orphans and lost children. This way the state will know there are no fraudulent claims being made.'

'I'll treat it like a case for the law,' Dayton vowed. 'Is that the help you wanted?'

'No, not really,' Knute said. He hesitated, as if uncertain of what he wanted to say. 'What I need . . . it's an actual life-or-death situation. This is . . . ' He shook his head and started again. 'Dee, let me tell you a story. After you've heard it, maybe you can suggest a way to proceed.'

'You're asking my advice?' Dayton didn't hide his surprise. 'You're the one who went to college and got all smart and educated.'

'This tale is about a young woman,' Knute stuck to his narrative. 'She was my client, but the trial was a complete farce, little more than a kangaroo court. I had no chance to win her case, and day after tomorrow she is to be hanged for murder.'

★ ★ ★

Ludwig sat in his leather-bound chair and glanced at the newspaper. It was three days old, having been sent from San Francisco with the mail. He specifically chose this paper because it included world news. Not that his family would ever return home to Germany, but an intelligent man liked to keep abreast of what was happening in the world.

Klaus entered their shared office and plopped down on the divan. 'What's new, dear brother?'

'Did you know there is a fancy dining

car on the Chicago-Alton Railroad? George Pullman is calling it the Delmonico, after the restaurant of the same name in New York. It's been running for almost a year.'

'Interesting . . . if we ever go back East,' Klaus remarked, unable to hide the fact he had no interest whatsoever. He immediately turned to a more urgent concern. 'I've been informed our Good Samaritan attorney is writing more letters. You know he sent off a wire to the governor to try and stop the hanging.'

'Governor Haight won't intervene,' Ludwig said. 'He has a full plate of problems without getting involved in a small-town murder case.' He shrugged off-handedly. 'Plus, I made a substantial donation to his election campaign. It will take more than the disgruntled mutterings of an attorney who lost a case to prompt him to interfere with the sentence.'

'All the same, I think we ought to run Garrett out of town. Let him do his lawyering someplace else.'

'The man has done a lot of good work for us, Klaus. He handled those lease agreements last year and manages the city business all by himself. We would have to hire three men to fill his shoes.'

'Yes, but — '

Ludwig raised a hand to stop Klaus from arguing. 'He only represented the murderer so that this execution would all be above board and legal. It's normal procedure for an attorney to file an appeal or two when defending someone's life.'

'I don't know.' Klaus was unconvinced. 'That Alyson is a pretty girl. Finest red hair and most beautiful green eyes I've ever seen.'

'It's her Irish heritage,' Ludwig said. 'Besides, Garrett has a wife and child to support; he isn't going to risk losing his job here.'

'I'm just saying — '

'And Alyson won't look so pretty once she hits the end of the hangman's noose.'

'You're the senior partner,' Klaus allowed. 'It was your son she killed. I'll let you be the judge of what needs to be done.'

'No one is going to try and stop the hanging,' Ludwig avowed. 'Otto and Erich are watching at the jail. They take turns spending nights there with Lynch. Plus, I told Erich to have Wolfgang and his men keep an eye on the town. With that many guns, no one is going to mess with us.'

Klaus cleared his throat. 'Uh, speaking of my son, he got into a row with one of our teamsters this morning. Looks like the man might die from the beating.'

'Dammit, Klaus!' Ludwig snapped, unable to suppress his ire. 'You have to rein in that boy. He's driven off a dozen employees with his belligerent attitude and bullying. I've had less trouble with my three sons combined than you've had with him alone.'

'Hans couldn't keep his hands off of the Walsh girl and got himself killed,'

Klaus countered defensively. 'That doesn't exactly make your boys angels.'

Ludwig's stern look cowed his younger brother, even though he spoke the truth. After thoroughly putting him in his proper place, Ludwig admitted, 'You're right. Hans and Wolfgang were a lot alike, and, unless you rein in your son, he is going to get himself killed just like Hans.'

'He's not a bad boy — got a lot of spirit,' Klaus excused his actions.

'Bullying people is not spirit,' Ludwig argued. 'Wolfgang uses our family name like a weapon and wields it over everyone in town. It's bad for our image, bad for our business, too.'

'I'll speak to him,' Klaus promised.

'Just be forewarned; if a judge somewhere issues a warrant for your son, we won't be able to prevent him from being arrested. We have our livelihood to consider and we can't survive if our town becomes known as a stronghold for thugs. We are the town elders and must set the example.'

Klaus submissively studied the toes on his shoes. 'I hear you, big brother.'

Ludwig watched him rise to his feet and shuffle out of the room. He knew Wolfgang was about as controllable as a tornado. They had put him in charge of their freight and shipping office. He didn't do any of the paperwork, but he oversaw the teams, drivers and wagons. Now the moron had possibly killed one of the teamsters. It was tough to get people to work for you if you beat them to death for making a mistake or mouthing off.

Considering his brother's visit caused him to consider Alyson Walsh. He was not happy about the idea of hanging a woman. The action certainly would not bolster their public image. But she had killed his youngest son, albeit the most spoiled of his children. He had no doubt Hans had been in the process of forcing himself on the girl. He had done as much and ended up in trouble twice before. Ludwig had handled both incidents with diplomacy, as well as a fair amount of money, to make them go away. However, Alyson had fought back on her own. She had stabbed him right through the heart. It made no difference that the girl had been defending herself. She would pay the ultimate price for killing his son.

2

Dayton discreetly watched the jail during the afternoon and formulated a plan. There was a sheriff and two deputies watching the town and going to and from the sheriff's office. When darkness fell he knew where all three men were at. The sheriff had gone home for the day, leaving him two deputies to deal with.

Dayton was ready when one of the two men exited the office. The fellow took a look up and down the street, then started to walk towards the nearest saloon, either to get a drink or have a look around. He didn't get far before Dayton slipped in behind him.

'Open your mouth, lawman,' he rasped in a hushed voice, 'and you're dead.' To prove he was serious he pressed the muzzle of his gun against the back of the man's head. The warning stopped the deputy in his tracks and he lifted his hands.

'Back into the alleyway, and keep your eyes to the front,' Dayton ordered, using his free hand to guide the man. Once into the darkened passageway Dayton bound the man's wrists behind his back with a sturdy length of rawhide. He then stuffed a rag in his mouth and tied it in place with a strip of cloth. Satisfied with his handiwork, he checked to see that no one was on the street. The few people still awake were inside the saloon, so he marched the lawman back to the jail and stopped his prisoner at the door.

Having been observant, he knew that the signal between the sheriff and deputies was not verbal. Two taps, wait a short space of time and then a third tap. Dayton had his bandanna in place and his hat tipped low to hide most of his face. He knocked twice, hesitated, knocked a third time and pushed open the door.

The second man on duty was sitting

behind a desk asleep, feet up on the piece of furniture, with his arms folded and his chin resting on his chest. He had not even been awakened at the entrance of his pal. Dayton quickly tied the first man to a chair, then awoke, bound and gagged the second. He pulled his chair over to his first captive and secured the two chairs back to back. Next, he used the pot-bellied stove and some twine to affix a double-barrelled shotgun in place so that it was aimed at the two men. He ran the twine around the trigger and over to the duo, then slipped a noose over their heads. After pulling the twine tight, he cocked the hammers back and eyed his two prisoners.

'You can see the strain on that trigger, boys,' he warned the pair. 'If either one of you makes a careless move, it'll be the end of you both.' Their eyes were wide and fearful. When they bobbed their heads that they understood, it was a very slight movement.

Dayton took the key hanging next to the gun rack and went back to the two cells. The young woman had obviously overheard some of the goings-on and was sitting on the edge of her cot. She regarded him with an icy scowl, perplexed and suspicious as to why a masked man would enter a jail.

As for his own reaction, he was mesmerized at the sight of her. Golden-red hair cascaded down about her shoulders to frame the most perfect face he had ever seen. Even in the dim light he stared agape at glowing emerald eyes, a petite nose and chin, and sensuous ruby lips. Had he been a great artist, he would have immortalized this woman on a canvas.

'Uh . . . ' He searched for words. 'Beggin' your pardon, Miss Walsh.' Dayton swallowed his infatuation and quickly unlocked and swung open the cell door. 'I'd appreciate it if you would come with me.'

Distrust caused her brow to tighten. 'What do you want?'

'I'm looking for a traveling companion with red hair,' he joked. At her darkening frown, he tried a different approach. 'Listen, missy. In spite of the mask I'm wearing, I can assure you I'm on the level here.'

'Certainly,' she said drily. 'Who doesn't trust a man wearing a mask?'

'Did I mention I'm here to save your life? And I can assure you that I'm a perfect gentleman.'

She hissed her contempt. 'I've never met a *perfect* man of any kind, let alone a *perfect gentleman*.'

'If you want to stick around here for another day they will sure enough put a noose around your neck,' he said, changing his approach to blunt. 'You can savor your doubts about me and be hanged, or you can show some spunk and vacate that cell.'

The logic moved Alyson to stand. She took a moment to smooth her plain cotton dress. 'Where are you taking me?' she asked.

'I figured to head for Mexico,'

Dayton replied. 'Can you ride a horse?'

The girl still wavered. 'How do I know this isn't a trick, so I can be killed during an escape attempt?'

'Missy, are you really taking such a risk?' He was growing impatient. 'You are facing a certain death at the end of a noose. How much worse can it be to cast your lot with me?'

The girl remained stationary and Dayton threw a quick glance at the two bound lawmen. 'We need to step lively, gal,' he said, prompting her to act. 'I don't know how long we have before that third lawman shows up.'

Alyson obeyed, quickly moving out of the cell. The two of them strode through the office to the door. Dayton paused to speak a last time to the deputies.

'You can sound the alarm by moving your heads a few inches, boys,' he said. 'But it's a mighty high price just to catch and hang a woman you know to be innocent.'

One of them grunted something.

Dayton shook his head. 'Watch your language,' he said coarsely. 'I'm escorting a lady here.' Then he opened the door and peeked out to make sure the way was clear. He pulled down his bandanna and led the lady out into the night to the waiting horses. She needed help to get aboard and didn't appear confident about riding.

'You didn't say if you could ride or not,' Dayton said.

'I can learn on the way to Mexico.'

'Just let Mabel have her head and she will keep up with me.'

Alyson didn't speak again until they had ridden a short way out of town. When Dayton turned from the main road and started to circle the town, she came up alongside.

'Where are you going?' she asked. 'I thought we were riding to Mexico?'

'I'm hoping those deputies heard me say that. While they are looking for pony tracks going south, we are going to be headed north.'

'Why are you helping me?'

Dayton looked over at her. 'We are going to buy enough time to get you a new trial. Knute is requesting the governor to intervene.'

'It would be the same jury,' she countered. 'Bismark owns the whole town.'

'My brother said he was going to request a change of venue, which means an unbiased judge would hear the details of how you were forced to defend yourself. An impartial jury is sure to find you innocent of any wrongdoing.'

'You are Knute Garrett's brother?'

'Yep. He asked if I could help him with a miscarriage of justice.'

'You're as crazy as he is if you think Ludwig Bismark will ever let me live. I killed his son; that's all that matters to him. You would be smart to give me a horse and point the way to Mexico.'

'There's a lot of dangerous country between here and there, missy. A good many men who have gone into the badlands were never heard from again.'

'But you've broken the law. Taking me from those men makes you an outlaw. And if they should accidentally set off the gun you have trained on them, you will be guilty of murder.'

'Only if one of them boys has a weak heart. I palmed the shells when I was setting the gun in place. It isn't loaded.'

He could hear the relief in her voice. 'You will still have to answer for breaking me out of jail.'

'I've got a few friends in high places. I reckon I can get around a simple rescue without getting my name printed on a Wanted poster.'

Alyson stared at him as if he had two heads. 'A simple rescue?' she scoffed. 'Ludwig will have a hundred men searching for us at daylight.'

'Then we best not waste any time,' Dayton said.

Alyson rode on in silence. She said nothing about being on a mule, nor did she ask why both it and Dayton's horse were carrying a goodly amount of supplies. They proceeded into the black of night and soon the few lights burning in and around Shilo were left behind.

★　★　★

Erich entered the jail and stared in stark amazement at his two deputies. His brother and Lynch both looked as stiff as a couple of fence posts. Bound together back to back, sweat beaded their brows from the strain of having held their heads completely still for several hours.

Erich moved quickly over to the shotgun, eased down the hammers and removed the twine. Then he swore in disgust.

'You boneheads! The gun wasn't even loaded.'

Both men started grunting through their gags, cursing and vowing endless bloody vengeance on the unknown man who had done this to them. Erich removed their bonds and the two began rubbing their stiff necks and taking turns drinking from a water jug to get moisture back into their mouths and throats.

Otto filled in his brother as to the masked man who had managed to outwit and secure the two of them. He finished with, 'I heard him whisper something to her about heading for Mexico.'

Lynch nodded his agreement and added: 'I don't think the gal knew the guy. She seemed real surprised that someone had risked his neck to save her.'

'That's right,' Otto agreed. 'She didn't go with him right off — thought it might be a ploy to shoot her during an escape. He had to coax her some.'

'Did either of you recognize the man?' Erich asked.

'Wore a mask and was a complete stranger to me,' Lynch said. 'Maybe six foot tall, dressed like an ordinary traveler, with common headgear and carrying a regular Colt handgun.'

'He was no one I've met before,' Otto assured Erich. 'I took a close look and would have known if I had.'

'So it wasn't Knute Garrett?'

Otto sneered. 'No way. I'd have spotted him right off.'

'And you think they headed south?'

'Mexico was what he told the girl when he asked if she could ride.'

Erich swore. 'The morning stage just came in and dozens of people are already arriving so they can be on hand for the hanging tomorrow morning. We'll never pick up the trail of a couple horses.'

Lynch offered an opinion. 'We can wire ahead and see if someone can stop them at a town between here and the border. That's a long ride.'

'I've a better idea,' Otto said. 'Rico Santana is in town with his two Indian trackers. They are the best bounty hunters in the country. If anyone can find this mysterious stranger and the girl it will be them.'

Erich grunted his disgust. 'Rico never brings anyone back alive. Our old man wants to personally see that girl hang for killing Hans.'

'Yeah, but like you say, there's a lot of people arriving in town today,' Lynch pointed out. 'They are expecting a hanging tomorrow.'

Erich glowered at them both. 'We have to catch the woman before we can hang her. I'll see how much it's worth to Father to have the girl brought back alive. Rico might be reasoned with, if there's enough money in it for him.'

'You're the boss,' Lynch acquiesced.

Erich left the two of them and went out of the office. He might be the sheriff, but his father was still the man in charge. He would telegraph every town for a hundred miles around and offer a handsome reward for Alyson. Then he would talk to his father and see if he wanted to hire Rico.

★　★　★

Dayton picked up an old wagon trail that led north-east. His destination was a farming community called Larkin-ville. He didn't stop until mid-morning, at a creek crossing. He watered and tethered the horse and mule where they could graze while Alyson prepared a meal of salt pork, eggs and potatoes. She turned out to be an able cook. Once the meal was ready, she ate everything on her tin plate with an unfeminine gusto. Dayton wondered how long it had been since she had eaten a decent meal.

'My brother said you came to America as an orphan,' he remarked to open the conversation, while pouring a second cup of coffee from the pot. 'How old were you at the time?'

'Seven,' she answered. 'I was sup-posed to be shipped to the prison colonies in Australia, but I sneaked away from the holding area. A crippled, elderly lady found me huddled in a doorway and bought me something to eat. She was traveling to America and offered me a chance to go with her.' She made a face. 'Didn't say that I would be indentured to her for the rest of her life.'

After a brief pause she continued. 'I had to wait on her hand and foot every day, but it wasn't all bad. She taught me to read and write and let me live in her house. It had a pump in the kitchen, wooden floors and glass windows. For me, it was like living in a mansion.'

'What happened to her?'

'I was with her about five years before she suffered an apoplexy. She died a few weeks later and I was sent packing. Her relatives took the house and shipped me off to work at a factory where there were a lot of other orphaned children. I escaped from there when I was fourteen and earned meals and shelter any way I could. I ended up in Shilo a couple years later and got a job working at the hotel. I've done laundry and cleaned rooms for the last three years. It was a lot better than working in that terrible factory or finding work day after day to survive.

Everything was pretty good until Hans Bismark took a shine to me.'

'Knute said he attacked you while you were working at the hotel.'

'Hans considered himself the prize bull of the territory. He chased after every woman in town, married or not. His father owned the hotel, so he had the run of the place. He began bothering me from the first day he saw me. However, he was usually off gambling or running around with his friends, so his visits were not frequent and I did my best to avoid him.'

'Until the assault,' Dayton commented. 'Knute said you had a knife?'

'Sometimes I had to deal with unruly drunks — miners, businessmen and cowboys who thought a hotel maid was no different from a fancy girl working in a saloon. I never had enough money to buy one of those guns women can carry in a purse. So I kept a knife with me when I worked. I had used it more than once to discourage some drunk who tried to manhandle me.'

'And you had to use it when Hans attacked you,' Dayton postulated.

'He had been drinking and caught me alone,' Alyson said, recounting the event. 'I fought with him and tried to drive him away with my knife, but he grabbed my wrist and began tearing at my clothes. I struggled against him and we tumbled over my cleaning bucket. He landed on top and knocked the wind out of me.' The girl visibly shuddered at the memory. 'I didn't know the knife had stuck him until I felt something warm and sticky soaking my blouse.'

She stared into the fire for a few moments before finishing the story. 'By the time the town doctor arrived Hans was dead.'

'Knute told me his death was accidental,' Dayton said. 'But he also mentioned that the Bismark family owns practically everything in Shilo.'

'That's true. The two brothers, Ludwig and Klaus, hire managers to run the businesses, but they control the town and most of its citizens. Of their four sons, the deputy you tied up was Otto Bismark. His brother, Erich, is the town sheriff. They are Hans's brothers. Wolfgang, Klaus Bismark's only son, is the town bully.'

'Well, my brother is a smart man. If there's a way to get your sentence reversed or a new trial, he's the man who can do it.'

'You are risking your life and he is wasting his time. No matter what a new judge and jury decide, my life is over, unless I get so far away that no one can ever find me.'

'The country is getting smaller all the time,' Dayton told her. 'The Continental Railroad has joined east to west and rail is being laid in all directions. Then there's the telegraph. They have lines that run almost everywhere. Your best chance is to stick with me until Knute gets some results. Once you are no longer a wanted killer, you can go to a new town or city, possibly change your name to be safe, and start over.'

Alyson gave him a blank look, as if he was talking in a foreign tongue. She had grown up alone, working like a slave and barely eking out a living. No family, no true friends, she had come to depend on her own wits for her welfare and survival. This man wanted to take care of her . . . control her destiny. A spark ignited deep within her. It caused her to flinch involuntarily. Was that because the idea appealed to her in some clandestine way?

'Let me go.' She renewed her determination. 'I can manage for myself and no one will know you helped me. It would be better for me and safer for you.'

'Missy,' Dayton replied, 'I've never taken a job I didn't finish. I'm not going to start now.'

The girl's attractive features became hard. 'I believe you are an honorable man,' she said, appraising him candidly. 'Your brother seems very sincere too.'

'Growing up, our ma made sure we didn't miss any Sunday meetings,'

Dayton told her. 'I know the Ten Commandments, but I figure there ought to be eleven — *Thou shalt not turn thy back on a miscarriage of justice.*'

'You should not be risking your life to help me. And Knute has a wife and child to think about. Standing up to the Bismarks is not only foolish, it's dangerous.'

'Right is right,' Dayton maintained. 'Knute mentioned a man named Socrates to me. Said how the man would not allow anyone to rescue him from an ordered execution because he had too much respect for the law.' Dayton shrugged. 'I have a great respect for justice, but little use for people who bend the laws to suit themselves.'

'But Ludwig and Klaus Bismark *are* the law in Shilo.'

'Only so long as no one stands up to them,' Dayton argued. 'And, if you are willing to put a little faith in me, I'll prove it to you.'

'Put faith in you, just because you rescued me from a hangman's noose?'

'I'd say that's fair-minded on my part,' Dayton said. 'If a man saves your life, even if only for a few days, shouldn't that get him a small measure of faith?'

'Maybe you were read too many stories as a kid and now believe you are a knight in shining armor.'

'In that case, you would be the fair maiden.' He went along with her scenario. 'What do you say?'

She didn't hesitate. 'I say the evil king will behead us both.'

Her delivery was made in a half-jesting tone, the first break in her icy façade. Dayton chuckled.

'In that case, you might at least thank me for keeping you company. You've heard the saying about two heads being better than one?'

'Never when it meant both heads ended up on a chopping block.'

'Reckon that would only be the case if you were preparing a large meal and needed to fix up two turkeys for the feast.'

'You're making a joke?' Alyson's nose wrinkled with her frown and she uttered a sigh. 'You are unlike any man I ever met before.'

Dayton grinned. 'That almost sounds like a compliment.'

His simper was disarming. Alyson was struck by the notion it was the most engaging expression she had ever seen on a man's face — part boyish charm, and yet masculine, virile even. It was unnerving, upsetting. Alyson swallowed the silly notion, feeling a hint of ire. This man had saved her, but that didn't mean he had a claim on her. She was not the kind of woman to be either coddled or dominated.

She strove to remain aloof. 'Actually, I have met crazy people before; I just never sat down to share a meal with one of them.'

'Sorry, no take-backs allowed,' Dayton teased. 'A compliment is a compliment.'

3

Lugwig glanced up from his evening meal as his eldest son arrived. The cook immediately entered from the kitchen with a plate, eating utensils and a glass. Erich sat down across from him, paused to pour himself a glass of wine, and discharged a breath of exhaustion.

'I sent wires down the line for every town to be on the lookout for Alyson. Be tough to hide a woman with her good looks and flaming red hair.'

'And Rico?'

'He took his two Injun pals in the other direction. Said they picked up the tracks of two animals going north. He is going to check with us through the telegraph at every stop along the way. If we get word that someone has sighted the girl, he will head that direction. I've already talked to the telegrapher and he will contact us at once if a message comes in.'

'Who do you suppose helped that murdering little witch to escape?'

'Got me, Pa. I asked around and no one is aware of any strangers being about. One of the town drunks said he thought a guy arrived yesterday morning with a packmule, but he was too hung over to remember anything else.'

'Did you send notices to the towns in all other directions?'

'Every one that has telegraph service within a hundred miles. I mailed handbills to the others using the stagecoach lines.'

Ludwig grunted his approval. 'We need to get her back before Knute persuades someone to overrule our hanging. There hasn't been but one or two women ever hanged in this part of the country. All it takes is one sympathetic judge and we would have to prove the gal enticed Hans to get him alone and then murdered him.'

'Be a hard sell for a jury, Pa. The girl had a spinster's reputation for never inviting a man's attention. She also looks about as innocent as a newborn babe. I doubt any unbiased jury would ever convict her.'

'That's the reason we need to expedite her return.'

Erich spooned some beef stew on to his plate before speaking. When he did so, he was careful to soften his voice to make it as inoffensive as possible.

'You know Hans was forcing himself on that hotel maid. He's been after her since he first laid eyes on her, mostly because she never gave the time of day to him or any other man in town.'

Ludwig glowered at him. 'She could have called for help; she could even have used the knife to stab him in the arm or leg.' Then rage entered his voice. 'But she killed him!'

'She claimed it was an accident.' Erich defended the girl. 'They fell during the tussle. You saw the bruises on her face and arms where Hans had hit and grabbed her. Besides, she wasn't strong enough to have buried the knife to the hilt, not when the blade actually went through Hans's ribs.'

'The why and the how don't matter, Erich.' Ludwig was emphatic. 'Alyson Walsh killed your brother. If it had been you, I'd be doing the same thing . . . hanging whoever was responsible.'

'I'd never force my attentions on a woman, Pa. Hans was a feral tomcat who wouldn't take no for an answer. Because he was a Bismark, he took what he wanted and to hell with the consequences.'

'He was my son and your brother.'

'Yeah, and Wolfgang is cut from the same bolt of cloth, even if Klaus is his father. We should never have put up with Hans doing whatever he pleased.' Erich challenged his father. 'And we better put a stop to Wolfgang's brutality, or he's going to end up dead next.'

'Enough!' Ludwig snapped. 'This conversation is over.'

Erich pushed back from the table and stood up, having not tasted the wine or taken a single bite. 'I'm telling you how it is, Pa. You don't want to hear it, but you know I'm telling you straight. Killing that girl won't bring back Hans, it will only serve to brand you and Uncle Klaus as despots, tyrants who make their own rules.'

'You are sassing your father, Erich.'

But his son stood his ground. 'No, I'm speaking the truth. And Wolfgang is going to get himself killed when one of our hired helps decides they have been pushed around long enough.'

Ludwig enjoyed the power of owning a town, but Erich was his son, and he had always been smarter than both of his brothers put together. Rather than continue to shout and try to bully him into submission, he took a deep breath and let it out slowly.

'Sit down and eat,' he said quietly. Erich eased back into his chair and forked a bite of stew into his mouth. With more calm than he felt, Ludwig gave an affirmative nod of his head. 'You are right about Wolfgang. I spoke to Klaus and told him to rein in his boy.

If Wolfgang can't behave, we'll find a job for him that doesn't involve him giving orders to anyone.'

'And the girl?' Erich queried warily.

'She was given a trial and sentenced.' Ludwig refused to budge. 'She is going to hang.'

Erich took a sip of wine before saying, 'If that's the way it has to be.'

'Yes, son,' Ludwig said solemnly. 'That's the way it has to be.'

★ ★ ★

Dayton considered himself a light sleeper. Because of his profession he had to be vigilant. However, he had been several days in the saddle before he staked out the jail all day. He'd had maybe four hours of sleep in the past three days. His eyes burned, he was jaded from the long night, and riding throughout the day. After making a sweep of the area and watching for anyone on the nearby road until close to midnight, he picked out a lookout point and dozed off. That was it. Leaning with his back against a tree, he had shut his eyes to catch a few minutes of shuteye. It seemed only moments later that he came suddenly awake.

'Sonuvabuck!' he muttered aloud. 'You're getting careless in your old age, Garrett!'

It was barely daylight and he still had his back to a slender cedar tree. Except his handgun and boots were missing, a length of rope was wrapped around his chest and upper arms, and his horse, mule and the girl were gone.

Alyson hadn't tightened the rope enough to wake him, but she had looped it around him a half-dozen times and tied it off on the back of the tree where he couldn't easily reach it. *That woman must move as lightly as a gnat wearing moccasins*, Dayton surmised.

Using his hands, he began to inch the spirals of rope up his chest and eventually worked it over his head to escape his bonds. Once free, Dayton coiled the lariat and picked his way gingerly through the brush and cacti to where they had camped. The coffee pot was sitting next to a cold fire-pit and everything else was gone. When he peeked into the pot, he saw the girl had filled it with water.

'At least you won't die of thirst,' he grumbled. 'Not until your feet give out and you end up as a meal for the vultures.'

Dayton took a moment to search for food or anything useful, but there were no wild onions or strawberries near by. No seeds or berries were in season either. As for constructing makeshift shoes, the nearby trees had no decent bark and he wasn't going to be shooting any animals so he could use their hide. With a sigh of resignation, Dayton hiked gingerly down to the road and picked up the trail of his two animals. Then he set out after them.

A half-hour later he saw where the horses had stopped. There, next to the road, partly hidden by a tangle of brush, were his boots. He discovered his gun tucked inside one of them. Alyson had not intended to leave him shoeless and unarmed. Also, she had left him enough water to last him for a day or so. Her reasoning allowed for him to safely reach a farmhouse or ranch and acquire another horse or other transportation.

Thinking of paying for rent or buying a horse, he checked his vest pocket. The few dollars he carried there were missing. He removed his leather wallet from his back pocket and found that his papers and the bulk of his money were intact. Alyson had only taken a small amount of money. Of course, she had a mule she could sell if she needed the cash.

Dayton, having passed along this very trail on his way to Shilo, was familiar with it. The main fork in the road was a few miles ahead. One road led south toward Los Angeles, straight ahead lay several mining towns, and to the north was Larkinville, the nearest settlement. He had no idea which way she would go, so he had to remain on the road until he reached the crossroads. If she chose Larkinville, he might just catch up with her. If not, he would proceed there anyway, purchase a horse, and start after her. The delay would make it much harder to find her because she would have a full day's head start.

For the next two hours he mentally willed Alyson to take the road north. He had warned her of the dangers of trying to cross into Mexico. Most mining towns had no lawmen, but they were full of rough and rowdy miners. She would be smart to avoid such places. He kept telling her over and over to take the road to Larkinville. When he finally reached the crossroads he scanned the tracks for several moments, then permitted himself a smile.

* * *

Alyson told herself she had acted in the best interests of Dayton Garrett. The

Bismark family wielded too much power to oppose. She was saving the man's life by deserting him. The rationale had a satisfactory ring to it, but she still felt guilty about leaving him unarmed and afoot. Like the proverbial hero, he'd risked his life to save her from certain death. He had boldly stood alone against a den of blood-thirsty villains and whisked her away on his trusty steed . . . although her mount had been a gentle mule named Millie.

She recalled his easy manner, beguiling smile, and the disturbing mystery and intrigue within his knowing gaze. He had made her feel safe and secure, yet vulnerable and helpless at the same time. Alyson had never before looked at a man and wondered how it would feel to be held in his arms, and possibly kissed by his lips. Dayton scrambled her strict regimen and caused her to experience amorous sensations over which she had no control. She groaned at allowing such thoughts in her head.

'Darn your hide, Dayton Garrett!'

she grumbled aloud. *What gives you the right to affect me in such a way?* For such an honorable man, that was downright rude and ungentlemanly!

It was still a couple miles to Larkinville when a crop of corn appeared alongside the road. Beyond the massive expanse she could make out other crops, of beans, potatoes and wheat. A short way further along and she espied a building that appeared to house a mill for crushing wheat into flour. From the sounds emanating from it, and a powder-like dust rising from an open window on the upper floor, she guessed the mill was in operation. Another half-mile and she came to more cultivated fields and a wide lane which led to a large, two-story house. Adjacent to that structure was an enormous barn and two long buildings with about a dozen windows each. Everywhere she looked, there were workers in the fields: most looked like children. She took special notice when she saw three kids standing near the road, at the head of a huge field of onions. Drawing closer, she could see someone lying on the ground, a body of very small stature.

Alyson rode her horse over and stopped a short way from the children. She could see that the one on the ground was a little girl of maybe seven or eight years of age. A boy was using his hand as a fan, waving it in front of her flushed face.

'What's the matter?' she called to them.

'Ruby complained she was awful hot and done passed out on the ground,' a slender boy, the oldest of the group, standing over the small figure spoke up. 'It might be because she's thirsty, but we don't get no more water until noon break.'

Alyson removed the canteen she had refilled at a stream crossing and dismounted. She looped the horse's reins around a stand of sagebrush and hurried over to the unconscious child. It took but a single glance to see she was suffering from both the heat and malnutrition.

Alyson carefully forced a few drops of water into the little girl's mouth. When the child swallowed, she repeated the process until the girl was roused to consciousness. Then, to cool her down, she began to soak her clothing, splashing enough water to dampen her upper body.

'What kind of place is this that they don't allow you to drink water when you're thirsty?'

'This here be the Larkin estate,' the oldest boy spoke again. 'You best not be caught giving any of us a drink, lessen' you want Mistress Larkin to wail on you with her riding quirt.'

'That's right,' the other girl warned. 'Mistress Larkin don't take buttin' in from no one.'

'This little girl might die,' Alyson fired back. 'Where is the nearest doctor?'

'He's in town . . . Larkinville,' the boy kneeling next to the semi-conscious

59

girl replied. 'That's a mile up the road.' He had a worried look on his face. 'Can't you just help my little sister get better so the mistress won't notice?'

'Your sister needs to be put to bed, some place cool, and she needs to drink lots of liquid.'

'No one is allowed back at the Yard House until the bell sounds,' he said.

'We have to get back to work,' the oldest boy spoke again. 'Be real trouble for us if we are caught standing around.'

'Standing around!' Alyson snapped. 'This little girl needs treatment.'

'She won't be the first to lie in the fields till the bell sounds,' the boy told Alyson. 'No one dares stop to help anyone, not if you want to keep your hide. We've already risked getting caught.'

'What about you?' Alyson asked the brother of the victim.

'I'm scared too, but I can't leave Ruby.' His eyes were misted with tears. 'I'm all she has.'

Alyson made her decision. 'Help me get her on my horse. You can ride the mule and we'll take her to the doctor in town.' She glowered at the two other children for refusing to help. 'Mistress Larkin doesn't scare me one bit!'

★   ★   ★

After walking at a good pace throughout the day and until well after dark, Dayton entered the edge of town at midnight. The first light he spotted was a yard lamp over a sign that read: Room & Board $1 a day. Being late, he hated to wake someone up, but his body ached from his big toe to the top of his head. Rather than seek out a hotel in the heart of town, Dayton chose to end his lengthy trek and get some sleep.

The Dexter House was impressive, two stories high, with four windows facing the front yard. There was a barn and corral to the rear and the front yard had a nice row of flowers and a wide, clear walkway. Inside the front door he discovered a dimly lighted lamp above a small desk. There was a coat rack and a board on the wall that listed eight rooms. Only one number had a name next to it. There was also a piece of twine dangling next to a written message: *Pull gently after 10 p.m.*

Dayton had to *gently* pull a half-dozen times before a blurry-eyed woman appeared. Probably well into her fifties, the woman tugged a heavy, blue-colored robe together at the throat and squinted through the gloom.

'Beg pardon, ma'am,' Dayton greeted her. 'But I am sorely in need of a room.'

She yawned, ran a hand through her grayish-white hair and waddled over to the small counter.

'Set down your John Henry,' she directed, pointing at a ledger. 'I'm the Widow Dexter and it's a dollar a day in advance.'

Dayton put down a dollar and four bits extra for getting her out of bed. The gratuity instantly prompted her to become more amiable. As he wrote down his name and home town, she frowned at his unusual baggage.

'You look to be traveling mighty light, Mr . . . ' with a glance at his name, 'Mr Garrett. No suitcase, no saddle-bags . . . nothing but a coffee pot. I've seen men sell everything they own to keep their hats or spurs, but never a coffee pot.'

'The rest of my stuff kind of got mislaid, along with my horse and mule.' Dayton flashed a good-natured grin. 'You see, there was this girl . . . ' and he let the words hang.

Widow Dexter laughed. 'Enough said, young feller. I'll give you the room next to the facilities. You'll find a spare razor, soap and towels in the cupboard. It's two bits if you want me to heat water for a bath.'

'Mighty fine treatment for those in need,' Dayton commented. 'I'm much obliged, Mrs Dexter.'

'Make it Molly,' she said, leading him to the back of the house. She entered a room, lit a lamp and turned it up. The cubicle was bare except for a bed, table and washpan. 'No frills here,' she informed him. 'Breakfast is usually grits, toast and coffee, but I always have honey and preserves for sprucing up the bread. Supper is promptly at six every night. I don't serve lunches and Sunday dinner is always leftovers from Saturday night.'

'I'm not sure how long I'll be in town, but I do appreciate your kindness.'

'Like the sign says, it's a dollar a day,' she reminded him. 'If you stay past noon, that's another day.'

'I understand.'

'Anything else I can do for you?'

Dayton had a hunch this lady kept abreast of the local news. He decided to confide in her and see if it paid dividends.

'That girl I mentioned was headed this way,' he informed her. 'I don't suppose you noticed a young woman ride through on a horse today? She had about the most beautiful red hair you can imagine and would have been leading a mule.'

The woman laughed. It wasn't a mild, controlled mirth. No, this was a belly laugh! 'You don't . . . ' She could not cut off her laughter. 'Sonny, this is your lucky day.'

'You don't say?'

'I was over at the general store when that gal come riding into town. She had a couple kids with her and went directly to Doc Brackenbough's place. A few minutes later I seen her march over to the sheriff's office and that is where she stayed. They locked her up.'

'Locked her up?' Dayton feigned surprise while groaning inwardly. This confounded woman was more trouble than the last five men he had brought to justice. He reluctantly asked Molly if she knew why Alyson had been imprisoned.

'Come to think of it, the gal had a price on her head.'

'What about the two kids?'

'They are Larkin's nits — a rather

derogatory name for what most people around here call the runaways and orphan workers on their place,' she explained.

'Then Mr Larkin has a number of state wards?'

She blinked at his description. 'Wards?'

'California doesn't have orphanages like a lot of other states,' Dayton informed her. 'They pay someone to take charge of lost, unwanted or orphaned kids until they are of legal age.'

'You seem to know a lot about it.'

He related: 'I'm actually trying to track down the missing son of a friend of mine. He was kidnapped by the Indians a couple years back. A number of Indian tribes used to make their living by stealing women and kids and then ransoming them back to the army or anyone who would pay. It doesn't happen so much any more, but it's possible a few people take advantage of that arrangement to get themselves free labor . . . and a monthly fee from the state to boot.'

Molly snorted her contempt. 'That sounds just like something the Larkins would be a part of. Mr Larkin is a tyrant and his wife — if she's ever caught in a rainstorm she'll likely drown, due to her nose being stuck so high up. Whenever they come into town they strut like they own the world.' She offered an unladylike snort. ''Course, their massive farm and hired hands do support much of this town. It's why our name was changed from Trespass to Larkinville a few years back.'

Although he had learned a little about Larkin, Dayton played dumb. 'They have a lot of kids, do they?'

'A couple dozen, maybe more. If you came in on the south road, you passed by their fields and small plantation. They sell produce to many of the nearby towns and miners' camps. They've also got a mill for grinding wheat, and quite a few cows and pigs.'

It had been dark on his walk so he

hadn't seen much of their place, other than a few distant lights. He returned to his original quest.

'Getting back to the girl . . . ?'

'I spoke to the doc after the ruckus subsided. The gal you're interested in brought in a little girl and her brother from the Larkin place. Seems the girl suffered from the heat and needed some treatment. The two children were in town for a couple hours before the town deputy took them home. As for that redhead you're after, she was full of fire. I mean, you could hear the yelling at the sheriff's office all over town. I reckon that gal didn't cotton to being locked up.'

'Do you know what happened to the horse and mule?'

'They are at the livery. You can probably get them back if there are a few belongings you can describe for identification purposes.'

'That I can do. I'll check with the hostler first thing in the morning.'

'Anything else?'

'No, Molly.' He displayed his smile. 'You've been an angel of mercy for me tonight. I'll forever be in your debt.'

She laughed and half-joked: 'Won't be no debt if you pay me each day.'

He assured her he would and she left the room. Dayton closed the door, rested his hands on his weary hips and stared blankly at the ceiling.

'Sonuvabuck,' he muttered aloud. 'Right back where I started with that red-headed vixen!'

4

'They found her, Pa!' Otto shouted gleefully. 'We got a telegraph message from the sheriff up at Larkinville. They grabbed Walsh yesterday and have got her locked away in their jail.'

Ludwig leaned back in his leather-bound chair, pushed back from his desk and experienced a grim satisfaction. 'That's good news. Can you contact Rico?'

'He should get the message when he reaches Turley's trading post. That's where he expected to be by nightfall.'

'Then he was going in the right direction.'

'Yep. Them Injuns of his can track better'n anyone I ever seen. They should pick up that little hellcat and be on their way back by tomorrow afternoon.'

Ludwig bobbed his head and turned

to other problems. 'What's happening with the guy Wolfgang beat up? Erich said he might not make it.'

Otto gave his head a shake. 'Man, I believe Wolfgang is about three shades of crazy. I mean, he lit into the guy for no reason, then he kicked him several times when he was down. Broke a couple of his ribs and it looks as if he'll lose the sight in one eye. I never seen anyone who was meaner or more dirty in a fight than Wolfgang.'

'Erich should have tossed him in jail. Nephew or not, it isn't good for the family name to have one of our own behave like a wild beast.'

Otto shrugged. 'I suspect me and Erich are the good half of us four boys. Hans tried to manhandle every woman wearing a skirt, and Wolfgang is 'bout as mean as a cornered badger. Good thing both of our mothers died before they saw what kind of kids they brought into the world.'

'Speaking of kids, Erich's wife looks as if she has gained a little weight.'

'He ain't admitted nothing yet, but I think she is toting a passenger.' Otto displayed a silly smirk. 'Looks like you'll soon be a grandfather and I'll be an uncle.'

Ludwig felt a twinge of excitement at the prospect. He had lost a son, but he might soon have a grandchild. Otto had always been the homely one in the litter and was not capable of more than basic thinking. He had never had a serious moment with a woman who wasn't being paid to be with him. Hans had been willing to sire a child, but not as a father. He was all tomcat . . . or had been. Erich was his one crowning achievement as a father, a boy he could be proud of. However, Erich was against hanging Alyson Walsh for murdering Hans. It was difficult to raise a son with moral principles and then discard those values when a situation became personal.

'Let me know when Rico reports in,' he ordered Otto. 'I want to get this dirty chore over with.'

'You got it, Pa,' Otto said. 'Should be this evening.'

Ludwig acknowledged his son's reply and Otto left his office. Looking at the paperwork spread out on his desk, Ludwig found it difficult to concentrate. He had been careful not to look at Alyson during the trial. Little was known about her, other than that she had arrived like a beggar a couple years prior and had proved to be a competent worker. Personally, she kept to herself. Someone said she was an orphan who had managed on her own for a number of years. She had lived at the hotel as part of her pay, was seldom seen on the streets, except when shopping at the general store. Ludwig acknowledged that the girl had never encouraged Hans to show her any attention. Far as he knew, she had never invited the interest of any man in Shilo. Nonetheless, her stunning red hair, radiant complexion, and resplendent gray-green eyes naturally drew the attention of most men. For her, beauty was a curse. He admitted that the blame lay entirely with Hans, not with Alyson.

But she killed my son! he reminded himself. There could be no reprieve for such a crime. She had to pay for his death; that was all there was to it.

★ ★ ★

Dayton didn't manage to get up in time for breakfast. He was too worn out and stiff from the thirty-mile hike. He finally climbed out of bed at mid-morning. After asking Molly to heat some water for a bath, he went down to the livery to recover his belongings and claim his horse. Proof of his claim were some letters addressed to him in the saddle-bags. He paid the hostler for the animals' keep and left them in his care until he needed them.

After a soaking that relieved some of his aches and pains, he put on his spare change of clothes and shaved. He had the dirty clothes under his arm when he entered the dining room of the boarding house. Molly offered him a smile and nodded at several slices of ham, some toasted bread and a dish of peaches.

'Figured you might be hungry for an early lunch,' she greeted him. Then noticing the bundle of clothing, she added: 'I'll toss those in with my wash for an extra two bits. Have them dry, pressed, and ready to wear by this evening.'

Dayton was immediately receptive to the offer, acutely aware of the widow's need to earn extra money. With only a single full-time boarder, she was likely strapped for cash. As they ate, Molly told him how she had been a school-teacher in Denver when she met and fell in love with her husband.

'He owned a freight wagon and twenty mules, and went to work hauling ore from the mines to the smelter. My man earned good money but we knew the gold wouldn't last for ever. When Trespass sprang up as a town, we put everything we had into building this boarding house. We were doing pretty good until the hotel was built and a couple of the mines closed down. That eliminated most of our regular guests and also the overnight travelers.'

She tipped her head to one side, obviously taking a trip down memory lane. 'Then my husband died and I was left on my own. I still get a few customers and Mr Nolan. He retired from the military and has been here for about a year. He has no one left in the world. He gave me twenty dollars to put away for his funeral.'

When she had finished her story Dayton turned to his own affairs. 'What's your opinion about the sheriff?' he queried. 'Is he an honorable sort?'

She laughed. 'He's a hired hand, a flunky for the Larkins, along with 'most everyone else in town. I've tried to believe the Larkins were not be as bad as the rumors about them, because they took in those orphans. But you say the state of California is paying them to look after those kids. That means he is doubling his money. Not only doesn't he have to pay for most of his field help, he gets paid for their keep as well!'

'Well, if the sheriff is on Larkin's payroll, he might be less than forthcoming about the boy I'm looking for.'

'True enough. If the sheriff butts in, it'll be on Larkin's side.' She eyed him thoughtfully. 'What is it you aren't telling me, sonny?'

Dayton might have said something about Molly calling a twenty-seven-year-old man 'sonny', but he let it pass. He had a task to perform, but now he was faced with an unexpected setback. He could ignore Alyson and let her be taken back to Shilo, but Knute needed more time to get the governor to intervene. That meant he would have to break her out of jail a second time and hope they didn't get caught. If he got the girl out, how could he do the job he had come here to do?

'I'm going to take you into my confidence, Molly,' Dayton began. 'After I'm finished, you can ask me to leave or offer to help.'

Molly scooted forward in her chair, displaying more wrinkles than usual because of the way she was squinting at him.

'Tell me.' She didn't hide her eagerness. 'I love a mystery!'

★ ★ ★

Sheriff Byers opened the door and put a questioning gaze on the young Mexican boy who delivered their meals whenever they had a prisoner.

'What's the bottle for?' he asked, ignoring the three plates of food and studying a half-full bottle of whiskey.

'The telegrapher said the men who are to pick up your prisoner tomorrow said to buy you and your deputy a drink.'

'Well, say!' Byers grinned at the news. 'We not only get a reward, but a couple free drinks as a bonus.' He laughed and looked over at Deputy Hancock. 'And we didn't have to do anything but lock that sassy wildcat up when she come to us to complain about Larkin.'

The boy left the tray and hurried away.

Hancock picked up one of the plates of food: they were all the same, venison stew and a couple of hard rolls on the side. He poured a cup of water and carried the food back to Alyson. He passed the plate and cup through the bars and she took them wordlessly.

Byers wiped out the insides of their coffee cups and poured a couple inches of liquor into each. Then he sat down behind the desk, gazed at the meal, and made a face.

'Stew again,' he complained. 'When we get that reward money, I'm gonna buy the biggest steak in town.'

Hancock pulled a second chair over to the desk and bobbed his head in agreement. 'Me too. We ain't et a decent meal in a month.'

'Still,' Byers said, 'it beats tending pigs or plowing fields.'

'All, yes,' Hancock concurred. 'We've

had some pretty rotten jobs since we quit mining.'

Byers lifted his cup. 'Here's to our cash reward. I'm splitting it down the middle with you, buddy. We'll be sitting atop the pile when that pay voucher arrives.'

Hancock also raised his cup. 'I'll drink to that, Sheriff.'

★ ★ ★

Alyson had eaten a little from the plate. She didn't have much appetite, seeing that she was facing a long ride back to Shilo the next day and being hanged shortly thereafter. She put her plate next to the cell door and lay down on the cot facing the wall. *I should have known better than to ask for help*, she admonished herself for acting rashly. The only thing lawmen had ever done for her was to run her out of town or stick her on a stage to get rid of her. Of course, that had been when she had been too young to work, before people began to hire her to do the chores no one else would do. They paid her less than anyone other than a Chinaman, but she had gotten by. When she landed a job at the Shilo Hotel she had finally been able to earn her own way. She'd had her own room and the pay had increased a little each year. She really thought she had found a home.

She suffered a renewed depression over the thought. Hans had attacked her and ruined her job, her future, everything. Men were such animals, every single one she had ever met . . . except for Knute Garrett. She swallowed a lump of regret. And Dayton.

It had been a mistake leaving Dayton bound to a tree. Both he and his brother seemed to be sincerely interested in doing what was right. Most other men wanted to woo her or grab and tease her. The Garrett brothers had not been that way. In fact, Dayton had asked nothing of her, other than allowing her to help prepare their meal.

He had saved her very life and she had repaid him with treachery.

No! She defended her actions. He intended to take her back for another trial. He claimed she would be set free, but who could stand against the might of the Bismark family? A drifter like him? His brother, who often worked for Ludwig Bismark? She had deserted him because it was her only chance to survive.

Her mistake had been ignorance. She had assumed the law in other towns was there for all the people. Asking the sheriff to investigate the deplorable treatment of the children at the Larkin farm had been like asking General Grant to change sides during the war and join the Confederacy. The lawmen worked for Larkin. It was the same as with the Bismark family, the same everywhere: money and power controlled the law. If only she had . . .

Alyson became aware of an unusual silence. She rose up on to her elbows and stared curiously at the two lawmen.

They were sitting at the desk with their heads on the table-top . . . sound asleep! Before she could form rational thoughts as to why they were snoozing during the eating of their evening meal, the door opened to the office and Dayton Garrett entered the room. She sat up abruptly, her mouth agape, eyes wide with disbelief. The man had come for her a second time!

★ ★ ★

It was after dusk, and a few lamps had been lit throughout the town of Larkinville. Dayton had peeked through the window to see if the sabotaged bottle of whiskey had done its job. The heads of both men rested on the desk and one of the two men was actually snoring. He had no idea how long the potion would keep the two men under, so he slipped through the door, grabbed the cell key from a nail on the wall, and hurried back to Alyson. In spite of the danger of the moment, he smiled inwardly at seeing her shocked expression.

'Getting to be a troublesome habit,' he whispered to her, 'my breaking you out of jail.'

'Y-you came to rescue me . . . again?'

He unlocked the cell door and pushed it open. 'I don't take a job and then not see it through, missy.'

She started to join him but he stopped her by handing her his spare change of clothes. 'Take off that dress and put these on. If anyone sees us on the street, they need to think you are a man.'

Alyson hesitated, but Dayton was turning his back and moving over to the coat rack. While she shrugged out of her dress and pulled on the too-large pair of trousers and shirt, he was selecting a hat for her to wear. He glanced her direction as she was tucking in the shirt.

'Stuff your hair into this,' he instructed her. 'It will help hide that you are a woman.'

She worked her thick mane of hair up under the lining of the hat and tugged the rim downward to hide much of her face. Dayton gave an approving inclination of his head, folded and tucked her dress under his arm, then led the way through the door and out into the near darkness. They kept close to the businesses that had closed for the day and crossed the street to avoid the saloon and hotel.

'How did you put the sheriff and his deputy to sleep?' Alyson asked after they had gone a short distance. 'I mean, they are asleep, aren't they?'

'A renowned thief and robber from back East, named Peter Sawyer, discovered how to knock out the victims he intended to rob. It only takes a bit of snuff added to alcohol and the person will pass out. I was careful not to use too much, so we probably only have a few minutes.'

'We can't get very far in a few minutes.'

'So little trust you have in the man

who has broken you out of two different jails.'

Alyson tipped back her head so she could look at him. Dayton could not help smiling at how dewy-eyed she looked in the large, floppy hat and his oversized spare clothes. He did not laugh at her, however, on account of the serious expression on her face.

'We have to help those children,' she stated. 'Several of them have died due to lack of medical treatment and not having proper food and shelter. Some have been put into a special room, a cellar or basement of the house and have never returned.'

'You're talking about the Larkin place?'

'Yes.'

'I was actually on my way to see Walt Larkin when my brother contacted me. Soon as you are tucked away in a safe place, I'll get on with that task.'

'But . . . '

Dayton shushed her. 'Don't be talking any more,' he warned. 'If anyone

86

realizes you are a girl, my plan won't be worth a red-eye bean.'

Alyson fell silent and Dayton kept up a quick pace until they reached the boarding house. They went inside to find Molly waiting impatiently. She had a washpan and soap, and a colorless dress was folded on top of the table. Next to it were a pair of scissors and a black horsehair wig.

'What are you . . . ?'

'Take off that louse cage and set yourself in the chair, young lady,' Molly instructed. 'We've no time to lose.'

Alyson gave a startled look at Dayton. He reached out and took her hat, then gestured for her to sit down.

'Molly is going to make you disappear while I make a false trail out of town. I know a few tricks and should be able to lose any posse that might come looking.'

'Yes, but . . . ' Alyson began.

Molly put her hands on Alyson's shoulders, practically forcing her to sit. Then she began to cut her hair.

'This won't be pretty, but there's no way we can hide all of that hair,' she grunted. 'Besides, it'll grow back quick enough.'

Dayton turned and went out the door, leaving the two women to get acquainted. He hurried to get his horse from where he had left her, standing at the hitching rack next to the sheriff's office. He was careful to scuff the ground to hide his bootprints, and mounted up. Once he was safely out of town, he put the horse into an easy lope. He would keep up the canter south along the main road for a few miles until he could swing east and make for a cattle ranch he remembered passing. Once among a herd he would mix in his horse's tracks and find a wash or creek, something that would hide the fact that he had turned back for town. With luck, he would not leave enough of a trail for anyone to follow, no matter how good the tracker.

★ ★ ★

Alyson almost shed tears watching the long reddish-gold locks as they were felled by the voracious *snip-snip-snip* of the scissors. Molly kept cutting until Alyson's hair was almost as short as Dayton's. Then the woman helped wash the remainder of her hair and used a towel to dry her head.

'I feel naked,' Alyson complained, running her hand over the damp stubble. 'You barely left enough to comb.'

Molly explained, 'Until Dayton gets things sorted out here in town, you are going to have to pass yourself off as someone else.'

'But the sheriff . . . ?'

'He won't get close enough to you to see your face,' Molly explained. 'With this black wig, a little beet juice and rouge to darken your skin, and these . . . ' She picked up a pair of spectacles. 'My husband used them for reading. With your hair pulled back in a severe bun, a tanned look to hide your ivory-colored complexion, and wearing the eyeglasses, no one is going to recognize you, not from a distance anyway.'

'Why are you helping me?'

'My husband was an honorable and decent man,' Molly said. 'Dayton and me had a long talk before I agreed to help. He seems an honorable and decent man too.'

'Decent and honorable? He broke me out of jail . . . twice!'

'He explained your situation to me, Alyson, and I agreed to help him.'

'Did he say why he was on his way to Larkinville before his brother told him about me?'

Molly explained about how some Indian tribes stole women and children on raids and then ransomed them to the army or anyone who would pay. She went on about Dayton contacting his brother, who then checked with several state agencies. That led him here, when the boy he was looking for was discovered to be at Larkin's place.

'I saw a lot of children working in the fields.'

'Yes,' Molly agreed. 'Larkin has gotten a lot of cheap labor by taking in unclaimed, orphaned or ransomed children. The state then assigns those wards to Larkin, until a relative is found or they reach legal age.'

'What the man does is make slaves out of those children!'

Molly displayed a serious expression. 'Yes, there have been rumors of . . . well, rumors of children who disappeared. Mr Larkin has claimed that one or two ran away.'

'It's more likely they died and he covered it up.'

'Mr Garrett will get to the bottom of things.'

Alyson gazed at Molly, amazed at the amount of confidence she voiced in a man she barely knew. Was her intuition that good, or was she gullible and too trusting of a brave, seemingly capable, and rather handsome man? Whichever it was, Alyson was not going to desert those children. Even as she wondered if she would recognize herself in a mirror when Molly finished, she was planning, scheming, working on a way to help Ruby and her brother Kenny.

5

Dayton arrived back an hour before daylight and put his horse in the corral behind the boarding house. Both he and his horse were worn out from the long journey. He took a few minutes to rub down his mare and make sure she had some grain, hay and water. Then he staggered wearily into the house and crept quietly to his room. Pushing the door open, he was surprised to see the lamp wick was burning. It was adjusted very low, but someone had lit the lamp.

'I've been waiting for you,' Alyson said in a hushed voice.

Dayton turned the lamp up so he could see his visitor, but he hardly recognized the girl seated on his bed. Her dark hair was pulled back into a tight bun at the back of her head and spectacles were perched on the end of her nose. She wore a long-sleeved, dark-colored dress that was buttoned to the throat and flowed downward to cover her footwear. She had tanned features and could have been anywhere from twenty to thirty years of age. If he had ever thought about meeting up with an unprepossessing spinster, this woman fitted the description perfectly.

'The voice sounds vaguely familiar,' Dayton jested. 'Are you somewhere beneath that disguise, Miss Walsh?'

'I have an idea,' Alyson said, wasting no time. 'You have to listen to me.'

Dayton uttered a prolonged sigh. 'I've been up all night, eight hours in the saddle, riding through about the roughest terrain you can imagine. Can't this wait until I get a couple of hours' sleep?'

'Sleep?' Alyson was incensed. 'How can you sleep while sweet little children are working like slaves, starved half to death, and treated worse than stray dogs? Do you know that Mrs Larkin enjoys hitting those helpless kids with a riding whip? We can't stand by and do nothing.'

Dayton lowered his head, his shoulders bowed from his arduous ride, and put his hands on his hips. 'Speak your piece, missy,' he capitulated, 'but I'm making no promises.'

'Molly says you are searching for a ransomed child whose relatives have come forward.' It was a declaration, not a question. 'Let me pretend to be a maiden aunt, seeking my sister's two missing children — Kenny and Ruby Smith!' Dayton lifted his eyes enough to see the excitement glowing in the woman's eyes. She rushed onward with her entreaty. 'Don't you see? I can take the two children and keep them safe.'

'Safe?' He laughed. 'You're one step away from a noose, a fugitive from the law.'

'So I'll find them a decent home before I'm taken back to Shilo. Anything would be better for them than staying at that terrible place. Let me do this, Mr Garrett, and I promise to be good. I'll do whatever you tell me to do.'

'Did you miss the part of our plan where you stay pretty much hidden away until Knute gets you a new trial?'

'You can say the children are two more whose relatives have come forward,' she persisted. 'You can take them away from Larkin and bring them here.'

'It's that simple,' Dayton said thickly. 'Just bring them here to the boarding house and put everyone at risk because you want to interfere with my job.'

'Your job?'

'This started out as an errand for a friend, trying to find his kidnapped son, who he believed had been ransomed by the Indians. But now there is more at stake than his son or those two kids you helped. There is a slavery ring operating, one that targets children, and I have to follow the trail until I find the lowlife maggots who are responsible. Larkin is a piece of the puzzle, but I can't show my hand too soon or the trail will dry up.'

'I don't understand.'

Dayton was too tired to keep standing. He pushed the door closed, removed his hat and gun and sat down on the bed. Alyson was quick to vacate it and took up a standing position next to the bedstead.

'I have a list of names, provided by the state. Larkin gets paid each month for the keep of thirty-five wards. Some time back, when I was searching for my friend's son, I came across a wounded Indian. He had been shot while on a raid.' Dayton paused to remove a boot. 'I don't usually go out of my way to help an Indian warrior, one who might well cut my throat in my sleep, but I took a chance on this man. He told me that Larkin was buying children from a couple of slavers.'

'Slavers?' Alyson queried.

'Dirtiest business since scalp hunters,' Dayton told her. 'They trade goods and weapons to the Indians for every child they steal. Then they deal with men like Larkin and sell the child to them at a handsome profit. Larkin, in turn, contacts the state agency for orphaned children's welfare and requests compensation for the ward until the child's relatives are found. The warrior told me that the slavers actually encouraged them to provide them with older subjects, kids who would be better workers.'

Alyson fumed. 'Then I was right! Those people are running a bondage mill and the poor children are at the mercy of a monster.'

Dayton took off his other boot and reclined on the bed. 'Yes, well, you see why I have to do this carefully. Molly tells me Larkin has several hardcases working for him, a couple of whom might not shy away from killing anyone getting too nosy. The slavers also require secrecy and would stop at nothing to keep me from tracking them down. I have to move carefully or I could end up dead.'

'My taking charge of those two kids would make no difference to your investigation,' Alyson persevered. 'I would stay out of sight and Kenny and Ruby would be safe from harm.'

'I don't cotton to endangering anyone, missy. If I get the boy I'm looking for, I'll put him on a stage for home. The same goes for anyone else on the list. But taking those two might arouse suspicion for both of us.'

Alyson stood silent for a full minute. When she spoke, there was a cool logic in her question.

'What happened to the injured warrior?'

'I patched him up and he was able to ride away two days later.'

'You risked caring for an enemy warrior when some of his hunting party might have returned at any time for him. They would have killed you before you could explain your presence . . . isn't that so?'

'It's possible.'

'Yet you stayed and helped him,' she insisted. 'You risked your life for a savage who would have killed you, and yet you won't take a little risk for two helpless, innocent children?'

'Wait a minute!' he retaliated. 'You're using the same words — helpless and innocent — that my brother used to coerce me into breaking you out of jail. How many times do you two think I'll be a sucker for some sob story?'

'I'm pleading with you, Mr Garrett.' Alyson softened her voice. 'I know what it's like to be unwanted and treated like dirt. It's the story of my life. You have to let me help those children.'

Dayton had never been comfortable arguing with a woman. A man was supposed to look out for and protect women and children. It made no sense to add further peril to this mission by giving in to the girl's request. He had put his life on the line for her twice to save her from being hanged. He didn't owe her one blessed thing. Not one!

'I'll see how the meeting goes.' He gave in weakly. 'If I can convince Larkin of my authority, I might be able to get those kids for you, although I have no idea how we can hide both them and you for any length of time.'

His concession caused Alyson to do something that stunned Dayton to his core. She came over to the bed, leaned down and kissed him on the cheek. She rose up at once, murmured: 'Thank you, Dayton,' and then made a hasty exit out of the room.

Dayton remained immobile, except to gently finger the place where her lips had touched his cheek.

'Sonuvabuck, Garrett,' he muttered to himself. 'I mean . . . sonuvabuck!'

★ ★ ★

Rico Santana was not happy. He stormed around the sheriff's office and scalded Byers and Hancock with a smoldering stare and acid-laced curses. The sheriff made a helpless gesture when Rico paused from the dressing-down.

'It ain't like we done it on purpose,' he whined. 'We fell asleep and the gal must have picked the lock and sneaked out. We found where she had taken a horse and left town, but we lost her trail a few miles from here.'

'Just like that?' Rico cried. 'You both fell asleep?'

'It was strange as all get-out,' Hancock said. 'Right while we was eating supper, we both nodded off and didn't wake up till the sun was shining.'

Rico took a look around and saw an empty whiskey bottle in the trash container next to the wall. He retrieved it and put it up to his nose.

'You drank this?' he asked.

'It was not even half-full,' Byers explained. 'Ain't no way we would have passed out from a few swallows each.'

Rico tossed the bottle back into the garbage. 'You morons!' he sneered. 'You were probably given a bottle that had some kind of drug in it.'

'A drug?' Hancock was shocked. 'What kind of drug?'

'Who cares!' Rico snarled. 'It could have been anything that would knock you out. You've heard about men being shanghaied and forced to work on ships, haven't you? It's been going on for a hundred years at clocks all around the world.'

Hancock skewed his face into a dumb expression. 'We was shanghaied?'

Rico regarded him with a blank look and then asked Byers: 'Which direction did the girl go?'

'I can show you the tracks,' Byers offered. 'The markings are pretty clear from when she left town and stayed on the main trail. But once the gal left the road, she mixed in her tracks with a whole damned herd of cattle. We circled for an hour but couldn't find a single track to show us where she went after that.'

'Get your horse, and we'll need to look at your deputy's mount too,' Rico instructed. 'You can take us to where she left the road. My trackers will check both of your mounts so they know what their tracks look like.'

'Whatever you want.' Byers was eager

to help. 'Yep. I'll saddle up and head down the road with you.'

★ ★ ★

'The runner for the telegrapher just brought this from Rico,' Erich announced as he entered his father's office. 'Figured you would want to know straight away.'

Ludwig sat back in his leather-upholstered chair and put down the paper he had been reading. He waited for the good news.

'What's he say?'

' 'Girl escaped during the night. We are on her trail.' ' Erich watched as his father's face morphed from satisfaction to incredulity. ' 'Will contact you when we have her.' '

'Escaped!' Ludwig bellowed. 'How could that happen?'

'That's all Rico wrote,' Erich said.

Ludwig sprang from his chair and circled the room like a caged puma. 'I don't believe it! The incompetent fools!'

he wailed. 'They had her in their jail and let her escape.'

'Maybe she had help,' Erich suggested. 'Someone broke her out of our jail too.'

'But the Larkinville sheriff said she arrived in town alone.'

'Well, she won't get far, not with Rico on her trail,' Erich said thickly. 'Him and his two Indian pals have never failed to bring back the corpse of the person they went after.'

Ludwig chose not to comment on Erich's assumption that the girl would be returned draped over a saddle.

'Time is not on our side,' he admitted anxiously. 'The longer that woman is on the loose, the better the chance Knute will find someone who will act on her behalf.'

'I can't say I'd be sorry, Pa. We both know Hans brought this on himself.'

Ludwig gnashed his teeth. 'We are Bismarks, Erich. We can't allow anyone to get away with murdering one of our own. Yes, Hans brought this on himself, but the fact remains he was killed by a bitter, man-hating shrew, one who could have used her knife to ward off Hans's advances, but chose to stab him in the heart instead.'

'You would make a good politician,' Erich said sourly. 'Spin the bottle any direction you want, Hans was going to end up dead one day. If not by Alyson, it would have been a father, husband or brother of one of the women he molested.'

Ludwig scowled at his son. 'This conversation is over.' He pondered his options while Erich stood in obedient silence. 'Send Wolfgang to see me. I have a job for him that will get him out of town for a few days.'

'Sure thing, Pa,' Erich said. 'I'll round him up.'

'Keep me posted on anything concerning Alyson's capture.'

'The telegrapher knows to contact us if any news comes in.'

'Good.' Ludwig hesitated, hating it when he and Erich were on the outs with one another. 'I'll see you later,' he said weakly.

'Yeah, Pa,' Erich replied. 'See you.' And the young man left him alone.

Ludwig held on to his fury for Hans being killed. Wolfgang would be glad to do the little chore he had in mind. It would get him out of town and save him, Ludwig, any more grief too. He thought: *It's about time my nephew did something besides give me headaches!*

★   ★   ★

Dayton rode up to the main house and stopped at the hitching rail. He paused to admire the well-kept estate. A cobblestone pathway led to the adjacent two bunkhouses, one of which was two stories and big enough to house twenty men. Several patches of flowers were along the front yard, with a neatly trimmed grass lawn surrounding three sides of the house. Not quite a mansion, it rivaled some of the nicest plantation homes he had ever seen.

He off-mounted and tied the reins of his horse to the rail. Before he could approach the front door a burly gent, controlling two powerful-looking dogs on leashes, appeared from out of nowhere. He held the pair of snarling beasts in check, the muscles of his thick arms bulging from the effort. He wore no hat and there wasn't a hair on his head. His mustache was thick and wide, set beneath a broad, flat nose, and he had suspicious, glaring eyes. What he lacked in hair on his head was offset by eyebrows that were as thick and gnarly as two vacated birds' nests.

'Whadda' yuh want here, mister?' he demanded.

'I'm from the governor's office,' Dayton said easily. 'Would you inform Mr Larkin that I am here to see him?'

The brute frowned. 'What about?'

'I'm not in the habit of discussing business with three guard dogs,' Dayton informed him curtly. 'Tell your master that he has an important visitor.'

Slapping the man's face would not

have produced a darker scowl. After a moment's hesitation, the man took the two dogs and disappeared round to the side of the house. Seconds later a middle-aged couple came out of the front door. They remained in the shade of the porch roof and scrutinized Dayton from head to foot.

Dayton also sized up the man and woman. She might have been pretty once, but she was past her prime and had been eating too well and too often to maintain a harmonious figure. Her hips had spread out like a pair of chaps hanging on a fence to dry and her upper body had become more corpulent mass than feminine physique. Heavy make-up covered a face hard enough to have been carved from granite, she wore a gaudily colored combination of green and yellow, and her mud-colored hair was pulled back in an unruly twist at the back of her head.

The man was fairly stout in build, maybe an inch or two taller than

Dayton's five-ten, and he also carried about his middle extra poundage from extravagant living. He wore a brown suit, with a white shirt and string tie. Upon his head was an urban-style derby hat that looked ridiculous, especially a hundred miles from the nearest big city.

'I'm Walt Larkin and this is my wife, Sheba,' the man announced. 'What's the purpose of your visit here?'

'Dayton Garrett,' he introduced himself. 'I'm here from the state's agency that oversees and reunites children with their relatives. According to our records, you have thirty-five wards you are caring for at present.'

The declaration caused the couple to exchange glances. Dayton glimpsed worry, apprehension and suspicion in that single look. However, Walt remained outwardly unconcerned.

'We have taken in a number of unfortunate children over the past coupla years. That's the truth.'

'I am to do a complete accounting of

your wards and I have good news for several of the children.'

'Good news?' Sheba repeated distrustfully. 'What good news?'

'A number of relatives have come forward or contacted our office, searching for their lost or ransomed children. According to our records, some of those kids are in your care.'

Walt nervously wet his lips. 'Well, uh, yes,' he managed with considerable effort. 'That is good news.'

'You said a full accounting?' Sheba ignored the possibility of a happy reunion of children and family. 'What do you want from us?'

'I need to see all of the children,' Dayton told her. 'I have to check their names off of the list. It's so the agency knows exactly where all of the state's wards are being housed, and it makes my job easier whenever a relative contacts us about a missing child.'

'The children are mostly doing chores right now,' Sheba said. 'Why don't you come back tomorrow morning and you can see them before they start the day's work.'

'I timed my trip so I would be here at noon. I'm sure you provide the three meals a day the state requires. I thought I might speak to and verify each child at their mealtime.'

Walt took charge. He stepped forward and called, 'Jammer!'

The burly dog-handler appeared at the corner of the house. 'Yes, Mr Larkin?'

'See that Mrs Young has the soup and rolls ready for the noon meal. Then ring the bell for the workers to come in.'

Jammer bobbed his head obediently. 'Yes, sir, Mr Larkin. I'll see to it.' Then he was gone once more round the side of the house.

Walt returned his attention to Dayton. 'If you would care for a cool drink, we have some lemonade, or perhaps a brandy?'

'Lemonade would be fine,' Dayton replied. 'I never drink hard liquor during working hours.'

Walt didn't invite him inside the house. Instead, he gestured toward several chairs on the porch, which were sheltered by the roof and shaded from the sun.

'Sheba, dear,' he addressed his wife, 'would you be good enough to fetch us each a glass?'

Dayton noticed him give Sheba a silent message, but he pretended to be looking where he was going as he walked over and sat down on one of the chairs. As soon as Sheba entered the house to get a couple glasses of lemonade, there came the sound of hushed orders and the rustle of bodies moving about. Mrs Larkin appeared moments later with the drinks in her hands.

Dayton again saw the married pair exchange looks in silent communication. However, he took a sip of the drink and found it was quite good. He mentioned it to Walt and the man informed him that they could get an abundance of fruits and vegetables that were not available in other regions due to the cooler weather.

They had nearly finished their drinks when a bell sounded. It was not so loud as a church bell, as it was obviously some kind of chime that was being struck with a hammer or metal bar. It echoed across the yard and into the nearby hills. Within moments, Dayton saw a couple men and numerous children coming towards the house at a rapid pace from several directions.

'The cook serves them around back,' Walt told Dayton. 'Do you wish to speak to the children now or after they eat?'

'After is fine,' Dayton replied. 'It should only take a few minutes.'

'If you will excuse us,' Sheba said tersely, 'I usually help with the serving.'

'Of course. Don't let me get in the way.'

'We have one child in the house,' Walt informed Dayton. 'I will fetch her from the special room we have for the kids who come down with an ailment or

114

suffer an injury.'

'Perhaps I should go with you to the child's room, so the little one doesn't have to be moved?'

'No, no. It's all right,' Walt assured him. 'She is due to return to her duties tomorrow. We are giving her an extra day to rest up.'

The words sounded caring, but Walt's gaze betrayed the lie. He was covering up for something; possibly he wanted time alone with the child to make sure she behaved properly. Dayton smiled as if he approved of the man's caring and benevolence, while his gut churned a dire warning. Something dark and sinister was present here. It was the same sensation one might experience when riding into a hostile Indian camp, wondering if you would ever get out alive.

6

After being left alone on the front porch Dayton walked round to where the meal was being served. There were rows of benches along two long, roughly hewn tables. The children were aged from maybe five years of age to several in their early to mid-teens. The two men he had seen on coming in were obviously overseers. They were served a portion of stew, with potatoes and meat, while the children got a bowl of bean soup and a single clump of bread. For drinking, the men had coffee while the kids got only water.

Dayton scanned the group and grimaced at the sight. They were a dirty lot, clothed in ragged outfits that did little to hide thin, undernourished bodies. Not a single child dared to look at him. The well-trained lot kept their heads lowered and eyes mostly on their feet, like an oft-beaten dog fearful of incurring his master's wrath. Once given their food, each of the boys and girls hurried over to the table and sat down. Then they ate as if starving, concentrating on the meager ration of bread and bowl of bean soup, until the dish was licked clean and the last crumb of bread had been devoured.

Upon a closer look, Dayton noticed a stripe-like mark visible on the shoulders or backs of several of the kids . . . evidence of being struck with a whip of some sort. Not a horse- or bullwhip, but something smaller. He flicked a critical glance at Sheba: *hitting those kids with a whip!* Alyson had claimed. A riding-quirt would leave such a brand. Not enough to break the skin, it would raise a welt that would remain for several days.

Masking his ire and disgust at the sight, he feigned indifference, as if the poor physical condition of the children was the norm. His attention was diverted to the child who had been inside the house, supposedly resting from a recent ailment. She was a tiny waif of four or five years of age. Sheba took hold of her wrist and whispered something in her ear. The girl's eyes grew wide and she nodded fearfully. Sheba gave her a nudge and the wee tot hurried over to get her bowl of beans. A fist seemed to close around Dayton's heart as he watched the pitiful child. She limped slightly when she walked, had long, black hair and somber, dark eyes. Once seated at the table, she spooned in the beans so quickly that she practically gagged on the food. She appeared even more ravenous than the others, and he had to wonder how long it had been since she last ate.

Alyson had not exaggerated one bit: these Larkins were monsters.

Dayton swallowed all emotion, maintained a poker face, and pulled the sheet of paper from his vest pocket. He had thirty-five names but a quick head count tallied only twenty-nine children.

Scanning the group of younger children, he located a girl's name on his list that fitted the description of the final arrival at the table. To do his job properly, he was not supposed to get personally involved. He was already crossing that line with Alyson's request. But — *dammit all!* — no decent man turns his back when faced with an atrocity against children.

The meal was over in a very short period of time. The young labor force sat obediently, staring down at their empty bowls, neither talking nor looking around, waiting to be ordered back to work. When Dayton stepped forward to speak to them, only one or two flicked their eyes upward, then were equally quick to return their gaze to the table in front of them.

'I'm from the state of California's child-care department,' Dayton began, approaching the tables. 'I need to confirm each of your names and ages before you return to work.'

A few children sent fleeting glances at

Sheba. She glared a silent warning with her eyes, but gave them an affirmative nod. Dayton noticed that, while Walt was a few feet away, it was the woman who held the reins and managed the children.

Beginning with the nearest child, Dayton checked off each name from his list, moving down the line. When he reached the twelve-year-old boy named Matthew Hamilton, he stopped. The boy was so thin as to be emaciated, with a shaggy head of dirty blond hair and hazel-colored eyes. He did not look at Dayton, but answered the simple questions put to him.

'If you have any possessions, Matthew,' Dayton said, after ascertaining the boy was the one for whom he was searching, 'go get them and return here. Your father survived the Indian attack. He's been searching for you ever since you were taken.'

The boy's mouth fell open in shock. He stared at Dayton in disbelief, then his face contorted and he began to sob.

'Dad . . . ' He gulped back the emotion. 'Dad is alive?'

'He contacted me personally,' Dayton explained. 'I knew your pa from back in the war. He and I shared a good many nights wondering about the next day's battle. He was shot up during the Indian raid, but managed to crawl into a ditch before he passed out. He was found later that same day and recovered after a few weeks. Soon as he was able, he began trying to find you.'

'I've got nothing worth taking with me,' Matthew said, unable to hide his eagerness. 'I'm ready to go.'

'All right. Stand over there in the shade until I finish.'

The boy hurried to the side of the house, still wiping at the tears of joy as Dayton continued down the row. He stopped again when he came to Ruby and Kenny Smith.

'Do either of you remember your mother's sister, your aunt Karen Tarkington?' (It was the name Alyson provided as that of the kindly woman who had brought her to the United States.)

Both children gave their heads a negative shake.

'Well, it doesn't matter,' Dayton continued. 'She sent us a letter asking if we could find you and return you to her. She has offered to take custody of you both.'

'Yippee!' Kenny shouted gleefully. 'We're going to a new home.'

'Oh, my!' Ruby joined in, her face breaking into a wide, beautiful smile. 'When can we leave? Right now?'

'Go stand by Matthew until I complete my list,' he told them.

Both children scampered away from the table and moved quickly to Matthew's side. All three began hugging each other over the good news. This was quite possibly the happiest moment of their lives.

Dayton progressed around the table, suffering a stab of anguish to see each child's hopeful look turn to one of distress when he couldn't tell them someone had come forward to claim them. The last child he interviewed was the little girl who had been inside the house. She raised her dark eyes enough to look up at him, but there was no hope in her gaze, only a deep sadness. Her pinched lips, her unkempt hair, the dirty smudges on her face and the exposed parts of her skeletal arms and legs, combined to make her about the most pitiful orphan Dayton had ever seen.

'And you are Debbie Queen?' he asked her. At her slight nod and total despair in her expression, Dayton's resolve melted like butter in a hot oven. 'I'm to inform you that your grandparents have put in a request to locate you. They want you to come live with them.'

'Really?' she barely whispered the word. 'I have grandparents?'

'Would you like that?'

Debbie ducked her head and barely murmured, 'Won't Mistress Larkin get mad at me?'

Dayton gritted his teeth but kept his

reply civil. 'No, Debbie, no one will get mad at you.' He tugged gently on her arm and pointed to the three rescued children. 'Go and join the others, Debbie. I'll be finished in a minute.'

Debbie wobbled away on unsteady legs as Dayton was confronted by a very irate Sheba. Walt had followed along like her pet dog, but he also sported the look of a man ready to kill.

'Are you telling us three sets of relatives suddenly showed up to claim our wards?'

Dayton did not reply to Sheba's angry query. Instead, he faced Walt and asked:

'Where are the other six children? I have to account for every child assigned to you.'

'A couple of the brats ran off,' Sheba answered defensively. 'We didn't have any luck finding them.'

'Plus, a couple of the kids died of illness or accidents in the past few months too.' Walt offered a lame excuse. 'You know how kids are, always getting sick or hurt.'

'I'm talking about six missing children,' Dayton proclaimed the tally. 'I'll need a full accounting for each one.'

'Maybe there's been a mistake of some kind,' Walt said. 'I don't think six are missing.'

'There's no mistake about the fact you have been receiving money for thirty-five wards each and every month,' Dayton insisted. 'The records here do not lie.'

'I've been meaning to send a letter and explain about the ones we lost,' Walt muttered dispassionately. 'Any extra money we've received can be subtracted from our monthly allotment.'

'Best dispatch that letter right away,' Dayton warned. 'Otherwise, the state officials might suspect you have been purposely defrauding them.'

Sheba bared her teeth like a rabid dog. 'You got what you wanted, Mr state agency man. Now get off of our property, before I have Jammer turn the dogs loose on you.'

Dayton grinned. 'It was nice meeting you too, madam.' Then he turned to the kids. 'Debbie and Ruby will ride with me. You boys will have to walk until we reach the main road. I have a mule picketed there, which you can ride on into town.'

'We best get out of here,' Matthew whispered. 'If Gant arrives, he might try and stop us.'

'Fillmore Gant?' Dayton asked. 'Man with white hair and pale-gray eyes?'

'That's him.'

Dayton led the way to his horse. He put Ruby behind the saddle, mounted up, then Matthew handed up Debbie to ride in his lap. Dayton didn't look back as the five of them started up the lane. He became aware of Ruby holding tight to his waist, and Debbie relaxed after a short way and leaned back so that his arms were around her. The boys jogged to keep up as they set a good pace.

Dayton, old son, he admonished himself, *you are mired in quicksand up to your lower lip and just took another step forward. Your heart isn't supposed to overrule your head.*

★　★　★

With the state agency man out of sight, Walt ordered Seeton to get the kids back to work. Meanwhile, Sheba told Collinsworth to stick around, and sent Jammer to fetch Gant, who was supervising over at the flour mill.

Sheba picked up the riding-quirt she carried whenever she was on the grounds. When she entered the house she struck the walls, the tables, the chairs, and anything else that was close at hand, cursing all the while. Walt tried to calm her, but it was wasted effort.

'Do you know what will happen when they start asking questions about the disappearance of six of our wards?' she blasted him. 'They will come sniffing around questioning the kids and our hired help.'

'No one is going to find them,' Walt

assured her. 'We can claim there was a mix-up of some kind, or that the missing kids sneaked away. The extra payments will be deducted from the monthly allotment and everything will be taken care of.'

Sheba gave him an impatient stare. 'For heaven's sake, Walt! You can't be so naive.'

'What choice do we have, dearest?'

'Gant might have to earn some of those high wages we've been paying him. We need to do something before that man Garrett can return to Sacramento and ruin everything. First thing, compose a letter to account for those missing brats. We'll write that there was an outbreak of cholera a few weeks back and several of the kids died. That will explain why they are no longer in our care and we shouldn't have to pay back any money at all.'

'What about the kids Garrett took with him?'

'Let him send them on their way. Once he's gotten rid of the brats, Gant can make sure he doesn't do anything that will hurt us.'

Walt scratched his head. 'Sounds kind of risky, dearest.'

She snorted contemptuously. 'Risky is letting that government snoop go back and report his findings.'

'Whatever you think is best,' Walt acquiesced.

★ ★ ★

Kenny and Ruby didn't recognize Alyson right away upon entering the boarding house.

'I told you I wouldn't forget you,' she greeted them warmly.

'Alyson!' Ruby cried, and ran into her waiting arms for a hug.

Kenny moved over next to her and asked: 'You gonna be our aunt?'

'Something like that.'

'Do you have to wear those eye-glasses and funny hair?' Ruby wanted to know.

'Only until we leave this town,'

Alyson said, drawing Kenny closer to hug him too.

'This is Matthew Hamilton.' Dayton introduced the young boy to Molly and Alyson. 'And the little girl is Debbie Queen.'

Alyson frowned at him. 'I thought Matthew was the only one you were supposed to bring back. How did you end up with another child?'

Molly Dexter moved forward before Dayton could respond, and quickly sized up the gaunt, dishevelled condition of the children. She squatted down and looked at little Debbie.

'You poor little thing,' she said, in a motherly tone of voice. 'We need to get you a bath and some new clothes. Same goes for all of the kids. Then I'll fix a big dinner for everyone.'

Debbie took hold of Dayton's pants leg and gave him a frightened look. He smiled.

'It's OK. You're safe now.'

'Well, bless my bunions!' An elderly man spoke as he entered the room, surveying the four children who had arrived. 'I don't remember seeing such a bunch of ragamuffins since the war.'

Molly gave Dayton a helpless gesture. 'I told Sarge about the situation, Mr Garrett. He volunteered his help, and you might need someone to watch your back.'

Dayton sighed. This business was getting more complicated at every turn. Rather than ask Molly if she understood the meaning of secrecy, he addressed the elderly gent.

'You're a little long in the tooth to have been in the War Between the States, aren't you?'

'Sergeant Jack Nolan,' he announced. 'Finished up my career serving under General Sherman. While under his command I was given a platoon to manage, along with some wet-behind-the-ears lieutenant.' He snorted his disdain. 'Dumb greenhorn got hisself shot in the first engagement. I ran the platoon after that. The War Department mustered me out when the war ended, under the mandatory retirement rule.'

'Molly told me you are pushing seventy years of age,' Dayton said.

'Shoved it right over the hill two years back,' Nolan said proudly. 'How-some-whatsoever, the local medico has done told me I've a troublesome liver ailment and won't see Christmas. That means I'm expendable if the job calls for it.'

'I don't want anyone getting killed on my account.'

'You need someone to watch your back, and a bullet would be a whole lot easier way to go for me. I'm asking for you to let me join up with you and Molly and the gal here in her clown costume. I've got me a bottle of laudanum to control my pain, a well-oiled Henry rifle, and a good eye for hitting what I aim at.' Nolan moved over and extended his hand.

Dayton took his hand in a firm shake. 'I accept your offer, Sarge. You can start by keeping an eye out for anyone snooping around. I imagine the

Larkins will be checking up on me, so we need to make everything I do look official.'

Sarge tapped Molly on the shoulder, as she was busy wiping some of the dirt from Debbie's face with a cloth napkin.

'I'll move my stuff to the upstairs center room that faces the street,' he told her. 'If you need to bunk one of the kids with me, that's fine. I can share a room while I'm keeping watch too, if need be.'

'Five of the rooms have two bunks,' Molly replied. 'We'll manage.' Then, looking at the children, 'Each of you is going to take a bath and I'll round up some clothing for each of you.'

'You start with Debbie and Ruby,' Dayton suggested. 'I need to talk to the boys.'

Debbie was reluctant to leave the room until Dayton reassured her that he was not going anywhere. Then Alyson sent Ruby off with Molly and Debbie. Sarge disappeared up to where he could keep watch. That left Dayton with Matthew and Kenny. He wasted no time.

'Tell me anything you know about the missing children,' he began. 'Did either of you ever see anyone escape from the Larkin place?'

'Never an escape.' Matthew was the one to answer. 'I heard of an accident where a kid got hurt and no one ever saw him again.'

'That isn't much to go on.'

Matthew continued: 'Well, I do know of at least two other kids who were taken to the basement. One was a little girl, maybe five or six years old; she was sickly and unable to work. The other was a boy with a club foot. He was so slow-moving that Sheba was always hitting him with her whip. Being slow wasn't his fault, but he could only weed a single row while me and the other kids would do five or six.'

'So those two kids were taken to a cellar in the house,' Dayton summarized. 'Did anyone ever tell you what happened to them?'

'I asked Mr Seeton about it one time — he's kind of slow, more like a child than a grown man, and he keeps watch over all of the kids — and he said that both of those kids were transferred to a hospital for treatment.'

'But you don't think so,' Dayton continued to probe.

'There's a plot of ground a little ways behind the house. It looks like a garden, because the soil is always freshly turned, but they don't plant anything there. After the boy with the club foot was taken, I kind of kept watch. The night after he went to the cellar, I heard something and peeked out the window. Collinsworth and Jammer were digging a hole. After a little bit they threw something into the pit and covered it up.' Matthew lowered his head. 'I think it was the boy.'

'But why would they do something like that?' Alyson wondered aloud.

Dayton could not keep the ire from entering his voice. 'You heard Matthew, they were poor workers. One was sickly and the other had a bad leg and couldn't move very fast. The Larkins cull the herd and discard any child who doesn't measure up.'

Alyson sucked in her breath at his explanation. 'B-but cold-blooded murder?'

'The hardships these kids suffer makes it tough for even the stronger ones like Matthew to work in the fields every day. When you add in a woman who gets a kick out of hitting them with a riding-quirt and practically starving them, it's a wonder they've only lost six.'

'Mistress threatened Ruby if she ever fainted again,' Kenny spoke up for the first time. 'She was real mad that Alyson took us to see the doctor in town.' He paused and gave Alyson an odd look. 'We heard Walt talking and he said you had been put in jail. Was that for helping us?'

'No.'

'So why are you wearing eyeglasses and how did you turn your hair black?'

Dayton fielded the question to save

Alyson the trouble. 'She's undercover, like a detective trying to infiltrate a gang of bad guys.'

'You mean bad guys like Mr and Mrs Larkin?'

'Something like that. You can't tell anyone that Alyson is here at the boarding house. For your own safety, if someone asks, you say that she is your aunt Karen Tarkington.'

'Aunt Karen.' Kenny repeated the name. 'I'll make sure Ruby understands.'

'What are you going to do now?' Alyson asked Dayton.

'It's obvious the Larkins have been getting paid for kids they've either disposed of or who might have died from an accident or illness. But a wealthy man with power and connections could lie about what happened to those children and get off by giving back the money and maybe paying a fine.' Dayton's features hardened. 'They're not going to get off that easily, not if I can help it.'

'But you have me hidden away,' Alyson reminded him. 'And you took three children under false pretenses. What if Larkin decides to kill you?'

'I'll handle it.'

'Mr Bismark will have men scouring the hills searching for me too. He will hire the best trackers and bounty hunters money can buy. They won't stop until they find me.'

'Knute will have your pardon or a new trial set up before they locate you.'

She looked at him as if he was crazy. 'How can you be so sure of that? Erich told me the governor didn't even answer your brother's telegraph message. Bismark is too rich and powerful.' Alyson laughed without humor. 'And you came a hundred miles to pick on another man who is also rich and powerful.'

'I can't turn my back on those children,' Dayton said. 'You were the one who said I had to get involved, even lie if I had to, in order to save Kenny and Ruby. Well, there are twenty-five more children out at the Larkin place. Someone has to help them.'

'But you now have the two most powerful men in this part of the country wanting you dead. Don't you think our best option is to inform the proper authorities, then grab the fastest horses you can find and make a run for Texas or the Mexican border?'

'Never learned how to run, missy,' Dayton told her flatly. 'And the proper authorities might take too long to act. I'm going to do what's right and put an end to this slavery ring and everyone involved. As for you and the kids, I'll see that you remain safe.'

Rather than argue further, Alyson accepted her fate. 'All right, Mr Garrett. You've gotten us this far. I guess getting killed is about the worst thing that can happen to you or us both.'

'Not exactly words of support, but it will have to do.'

'So I ask you again,' Alyson reiterated, 'what do you intend to do now?'

139

'First thing, I put Matthew on tomorrow's stagecoach and get him headed for home. I'll wire his father that he is on his way and the man will find a way to meet him.' He grinned at Alyson. 'That only leaves four of you to worry about.'

7

The morning meal was like a wonderful dream for the kids. The four of them were laughing and smiling, sitting at the breakfast table until they could not eat another bite. Molly catered to them like a doting grandmother and little Debbie insisted on sitting next to Dayton. In fact, she went everywhere he did, standing next to him, following him around the boarding house and coyly climbing on to his lap if he happened to sit down. Alyson had her hands full with the other three. Molly picked up new clothing for the kids from the general store. Matthew's were a little large on him, but he would grow into them. Next, Molly trimmed his and Kenny's hair, while Alyson used a brush to comb out the tangles of Debbie's and Ruby's hair. The four children soon looked like normal, albeit undernourished, kids.

Seeking any information he could glean from Matthew, Dayton asked about the men working at the large farm. The boy knew very little about the men at the mill, but he did offer some help when talking about the four who were often around the main house.

Gant, in his words, was scary; Jammer kept to himself but had control of the two guard dogs; and Collinsworth was Walt and Sheba's right-hand man. Seeton was the one he knew best. He oversaw the kids and even stayed in the building they called the Yard House, where all of the children slept. He was the one responsible for keeping the children working.

'He does what he's told and makes sure we all do our share,' Matthew finished. 'He moves around from field to field and jots down how much each of us does.'

'You mean he keeps a journal of some kind?' Dayton asked.

'Yes. He had me help him a time or

two, because he got behind and wanted to get everything written down for Mistress Sheba. He takes the notes he has scribbled down in his log book and transfers the weekly totals to a sheet of paper. Then he gives the page to Mistress Sheba. That way she knows how much each of the workers are doing.'

Dayton felt a tingle of excitement. 'But he keeps his own records too?'

'The scribbled copy, yes,' Sheldon said. 'He carries a small book with him all the time.'

'And you said Seeton was not a bad sort?'

'Only if Mistress Sheba gets after him to make us work harder or faster. With him being in the Yard House with us kids, he's the one we ask for new shoes or blankets. He also tended to our scratches or cuts . . . that sort of thing.'

'Do you think he knows anything about the missing children?'

Matthew shook his head. 'Only to mark down the day they stopped working in the fields. It's like I told you, he thinks the kids who are taken to the house get sent to a hospital. I asked him once if they ever came back from there and he said they must have been real sick, 'cause they never returned.'

'Thanks, Matt,' Dayton said. 'You've given me a place to start when it comes to looking for evidence.'

'You believe all of those missing kids are dead, don't you.'

It wasn't a question, but Dayton answered, 'Yes.'

Matthew lowered his head sorrowfully and muttered: 'Me too.'

Dayton had to get things organized and needed to get started. His heartstrings were tugged mightily when he left. Debbie hugged him and her eyes filled with tears as he started to walk away. He swallowed the emotion, but his chest grew tight at the way she looked at him with such a sad and imploring little face. He promised her he would be back as soon as he could and went down the street to the general store, which also housed the town's telegraph.

Salty Snyder, a slender man in his thirties, with a wife and three kids, was the proprietor and telegrapher, but Dayton couldn't trust anyone with the messages he wanted sent.

'You want to do what?' Salty was not enthusiastic about his proposition.

'I want you to connect me with Sacramento and then give me some privacy. I often used a telegraph during the war. I'll pay you five dollars to let me send my own message.'

'Wa'al, I dunno,' Salty said, scratching the thinning hair on his head. 'That ain't the way things is usually done.'

'All right. Ten dollars, but I require complete privacy.'

Money had a way of loosening the principles of most businessmen. Salty gave a bob of his head and led the way to the telegraph. He tapped open the line, took the money and, as there were no customers in the store, went out the front door to roll a smoke.

Dayton had listened to how he opened the line. As soon as he had sent the message to Sacramento, he opened a new contact with Shilo. He tapped out a message for Knute and signed it Grandpa Moses, a joke between him and his brother. Lastly, he transmitted a telegraph message to Matthew's father and gave him the stage information. Finished, he went out of the store and stopped alongside Salty. It was then that he noticed a man was watching him from across the street.

'I need a ticket for the stage,' he said to Salty. 'I reckon that's done at the Transfer and Storage?'

'My brother-in-law runs it, but he is off visiting my wife's uncle. The man has consumption and likely won't make it another week.'

'Sorry to hear that,' Dayton said. 'Who is selling tickets for the stage?'

Salty grinned. 'That would be me.'

'I hope you're teaching your kids the business,' Dayton said. 'If anything should happen to you the whole town would likely close down.'

Salty laughed. 'You leaving town on the stage?'

'Not me.' He told the man about Matthew and his father. 'I need a ticket to Denver, Colorado. Mr Hamilton will meet the boy along the route and accompany him home.'

'Molly mentioned you had a few kids over at her place,' Salty replied. 'She was here buying clothes and shoes for the lot of them. I don't usually give people credit, but being as it was for those orphans . . . ' He let the sentence hang, obviously proud of lending a hand to the unfortunates.

'Molly is an angel,' Dayton replied. 'I'll square her account when you sell me the stage pass. What time is it due?'

Salty beamed at the news, likely having figured he would end up donating the outfits.

'We call the eastbound coach the noon stage, but it seldom gets here before three or four in the afternoon.'

'I'll have the boy ready at noon

. . . just in case.'

The two of them returned inside the store. Dayton paid for the stage, took care of Molly's bill, and bought a few sugar sticks for the kids. When he left the store he again caught sight of a gent watching him. As he was staying in the shadows, wearing his hat low to shade his eyes, it was difficult to determine what the man looked like. He was dressed in work clothes, but his gun was low on his left hip. Other than that, Dayton could tell little about him. However, it was probable he was working for Larkin. The man had wasted no time putting someone on him.

* * *

It was sundown when Gant arrived back at the Larkin place. He sat down to a cool glass of home-made beer and told Walt and Sheba what he had learned.

'So the Hamilton boy left on the

stage,' Walt summed up when he had finished. 'I wonder what kind of arrangement he has made for the other three?'

'They are all staying at Molly's boarding house. Some dark-haired spinster type is helping her look after the children. Never seen her before.'

'Must be one of the relatives,' Walt opined.

Sheba had no interest in the children. 'What messages did Garrett send from the store? Did he contact the Sacramento office?'

'No way of knowing,' Gant answered. 'He paid Salty to let him send his own messages. He might have contacted anyone.'

Sheba swore. 'That's just fine! We don't know what the hell the man is doing.'

'You want me to scare him off?' Gant asked.

'I want him dead,' Sheba wailed. 'Garrett can ruin everything we've worked for all our lives. He's too dangerous to live.'

Walt looked stricken. 'He's an official from the state government, dearest. Murdering him might bring a host of lawmen down here. We don't want that.'

'There's no reason anyone would look in our direction,' she countered. 'We gave up the four mongrels without complaint. Far as anyone knows, we were happy about relatives finding their kids.'

Walt scratched his chin. 'Sheba has a point. With the oldest boy gone, there's only the three youngsters to tell anyone about the few names that are missing from the list. I doubt any of them really know all that much.'

His wife nodded furiously, eager to find a solution to Garrett's meddling. 'The man is carrying quite a bit of money,' she stated. 'You said he paid for the stage ticket, bought clothes and such for the kids and bribed Salty to let him send his own telegraph message. A man flashing that much cash is asking for trouble.'

'I doubt he'll go out after dark,' Gant said. 'Molly is supposed to be a pretty good cook and he is rooming at her boarding house.'

'I've been in the boarding house before,' Sheba said. 'I recall there's a board on the wall where she writes the names of her guests, and also what room they are in.'

'You want me to kill the man in his sleep?'

Sheba regarded Gant with a cool look. 'Unless you can think of some other way. Kill him quietly and steal his money and any papers you find. That way, the list of missing kids will be gone and no one at the state agency will be any the wiser.'

'I'll slip in about midnight and take care of it,' Gant said.

Sheba said, 'Good,' and glanced at Walt. The man behaved in his usual way and held his tongue. When Sheba was on the warpath, no one got in her way.

Wolfgang found the sheriff and deputy eating at Hattie's Eatery. He introduced himself, pulled up a chair and joined them. After the two lawmen gave him their names, he informed them he had come to join in the search for the escaped prisoner.

When he'd finished, he said, 'Where do I find Rico and his two trackers?'

'North-east of here a few miles,' Byers told him. 'Leastways, that's where we left them. They are making circles around where a herd of cattle had been grazing for a spell. Your friend claimed they wouldn't quit until they found the tracks of that she-cat who got away from us.'

'They've been circling all this time?'

'Big area,' Hancock advised him. 'Must be several hundred acres where the herd was grazing when we lost the tracks. Rico said the Injuns work on foot, so it probably takes a half-day to make a circle one time

152

around that much ground.'

'When they finish a circle they move out a hundred yards or so and go around again,' Byers took over. 'Hell, it could take them a week to find any tracks. I reckon that gal is in Utah by now.'

'I don't get it,' Wolfgang said. 'Alyson worked as a maid at a hotel. I doubt she ever did much riding. Where would she learn about hiding her horse's trail?'

Byers told him about the bottle of whiskey and how they had probably been knocked out.

'So she had help,' Wolfgang surmised. 'That's twice someone has gotten her out of jail.'

'But there was just one set of tracks leaving town,' the sheriff said. 'Rico agreed the prints weren't deep enough for the horse to have been carrying double.'

'You two been keeping an eye out for her in town?'

Byers laughed. 'We'd have spotted that feline in a second. She sure enough lit out. But, you have a point, Bismark. It could be that we were tracking her pal and not her. He could be the one who knows how to lose a posse.'

'Any strangers come through the day of the jail breakout?'

'No more'n usual,' Byers said. 'The only guy who has been here since before the escape has a job checking on kids who are wards of the state. There's also a dark-haired woman who showed up to fetch a couple of those orphan kids. Both of them are staying at Widow Dexter's boarding house, there at the edge of town.'

'No one else?'

'Might want to check at the hotel; most of their customers only stay for a night or two. We don't check on every customer they get.'

'I'll be staying at the hotel tonight,' Wolfgang decided. 'I'll ask around when I turn in. Tomorrow, I'll ride out and find Rico. Is this the best place in town to eat?'

'They serve good food if you can

afford it. We get our meals free, but nothing other than the daily specials they put out. Anything extra costs us money.'

Wolfgang motioned to the elderly woman who was taking orders and bringing out the meals. He ordered the best steak in the house and smiled to himself when both Byers and Hancock groaned. They were finishing their meal — a bowl of chili and a wedge of wheat bread.

* * *

Dayton was removing a boot when a soft tap came at his door. He said, 'Yeah?' and Alyson entered the room. She appeared unsure of herself, hands clasped together and her head lowered to hide her eyes.

'The children are in bed for the night,' she murmured softly, as if they were next door and her voice might disturb their sleep. 'Kenny and his sister are in one room and Debbie is bedded down next to my room.'

'Good.' He spoke the single word and waited. Alyson appeared to have something else she wanted to say. It wouldn't have been necessary to enter his bedroom just to tell him the obvious, unless she was worried he would not approve of the sleeping arrangements. That didn't seem likely.

'I . . . ' she began, but then lost her nerve and blurted: 'I shouldn't have troubled you. This whole thing — you taking in these kids, rescuing me . . . I don't . . . ' But she did not finish.

'Missy,' Dayton decided to take some pressure off her conscience, 'I was on my way here to get Matthew before Knute told me about your situation. You didn't force me to do anything I didn't choose to do.'

That statement caused her head to lift. Although she was not wearing the eyeglasses, Alyson did have on the fake black hair. Bundled so tightly, with her complexion darkened with the special formula Molly had concocted, it made her look plain. However, he had seen the way her flowing red-gold hair highlighted the creamy-pink hue of her complexion. Beneath her disguise, she was the most beautiful woman he had ever seen.

His evaluation must have shown in his face because Alyson stepped back uncertainly. Her lips parted as if to speak, but no words were forthcoming. Dayton quickly suppressed his desire, aware of how many times this young lady must have been forced to ward off unwanted attention. He would not allow himself to take advantage of the fact that she was indebted to him for his help. It took all of his willpower, but he averted his gaze and began to remove his second boot.

'Was there anything else?' he asked, purposely casual.

Alyson didn't answer for a few seconds, as if battling with another problem or dubiety. Then she backed up to the door and said, 'No. Nothing.'

Dayton wondered if he detected a

trace of anger or disappointment in her voice, but glanced up too late. She had whirled about and retreated from the room. It left him with mixed feelings and a thousand questions. He had no idea how he should have handled the situation, but he had obviously botched the encounter.

'Durned if you do, durned if you don't, and durned if you do nothing,' he muttered. Some things had never changed for him. Women had always posed special problems with which he hadn't the faintest clue as to how to deal.

★ ★ ★

Alyson opened the children's doors and peeked in to see they were in bed. Then she went to her own room and removed the uncomfortable wig and clothing. She had a nightdress that Molly had provided for her. It was much too large, being that it had belonged to and been left behind by one of Molly's rather large guests. She put out the lamp and climbed into bed.

Staring at the dark ceiling, she went over the episode with Dayton. First, she cursed herself for going to see a man in his bedroom. It was brash, impetuous, foolhardy even. What had she expected? Indeed, what had she wanted to happen? A warm flush flooded her cheeks at the notion. Had she expected to end up in the man's arms? Have him kiss her? Had that been what she wanted?

Alyson groaned her chagrin. She had seen the look of desire enter Dayton's eyes. It had been what she wanted to see, but it frightened her too. She had never intentionally enticed a man, never actually flirted with one. Had she been too coy? Or had she been too bold? Should she have said something about him being the first man she had ever trusted with her life? That he made her feel safe? That she wanted to have more than a casual relationship with him?

'Heavens no!' she muttered aloud.

Honesty was something that came naturally to Alyson . . . at least with herself. She knew men chased after her because she was pretty. She hated to be candidly vain, but she was aware that she stood out among most women. It wasn't only her hair, she was petite in build and had delicate features. Her flawless complexion and deep-grayish-green eyes enhanced her comeliness. Added to that, she maintained an air of aloofness that many men assumed was a challenge.

Inside, Alyson was ambivalent, fearful of amorous notions or unleashed emotion. She was a little girl, one who had gone unloved for so long she desperately wanted someone to cherish, someone to share her life with. Unfortunately, she was equally afraid to enter into a relationship that might fail or destroy what little self-confidence she had.

'Was it me?' she wondered aloud. 'Did I make a mess of things by going to Dayton's room?'

Alyson closed her eyes, feeling the sting of tears rushing to the surface. She pinched the eyelids tightly to prevent that from happening. She had not cried since her mother died. Karen Tarkington had brought her to America and she had left her childhood behind. She had been forced to be strong and self-reliant all of her life. There was no one she could trust but herself.

The vow seemed appropriate, but she knew it was not the whole truth. She was dependent on Dayton. Even if he had misunderstood and inadvertently spurned her pitiful advance, she had put her faith in him. She trusted he would save the children, and he would save her as well.

★ ★ ★

Dayton had barely closed his eyes when the door creaked open. He grabbed his gun and rolled off on to the floor, ready to kill or be killed.

'Mr Garrett?' a tiny voice squeaked

from the dimly lit hallway. 'Did you fall out of bed?'

Dayton jumped to his feet, harrumphed awkwardly, and pitched the gun on to the bunk.

'Uh, you surprised me, Squirt. I thought something might be the matter and was grabbing for my boots.'

The small figure, clad in a sleeping gown much too large for her diminutive form, hurried over to him. Her bare feet were noiseless, and the moon cast just enough light through the room's solitary window for Dayton to see that Debbie had her arms folded. He looked down at the upturned face and his heart dissolved in his chest. If there was anything more precious than a little girl, he couldn't imagine what it could be.

'I'm scared,' Debbie murmured softly. 'I dreamed Mistress came to get me. I cried for you, but you didn't come.'

'You know I'm right here,' he tried to assure her. 'I wouldn't let anyone take you away.'

'Yes.' Her voice was barely audible. 'But I'm scared.'

'What can I do to help?' he asked. 'We both need to get some sleep.'

'Can I sleep with you?' she queried, her plea undoing his last shred of discipline or logic.

Dayton looked around, even though he knew the contents of the room. He couldn't very well sleep on the floor, and the single cot was too small to share. He made his decision and quickly collected his clothes and gun.

'We'll go to your room,' he offered. 'There are two beds. We can sleep in the same room and then you won't have to be frightened.' He put everything in one arm so he could sweep Debbie up in his other one. 'That ought to take care of those naughty old nightmares.'

'Uh-huh,' she said, timorously slipping her arms about his neck. 'I guess that will be OK.'

The door to Debbie's room was open, so Dayton dropped his belongings on the unused bed and carried

Debbie over to her own. He gently tucked her in and was ready to leave her side when she asked:

'Mr Garrett, will you be my daddy?'

Dayton felt a lump form in his throat at the sincere plea. He had to swallow before he could attempt to answer.

'There are a lot of children still out at the Larkin place,' he said, evading any direct answer. 'You wouldn't want me to leave them there, would you?'

Debbie sniffed. 'I guess not.'

'I promise I'll take care of you until we find you a nice home.'

'I don't have no home,' she whimpered. 'Mommy and Daddy died from fever. I was left at the church. A man took me away and put me in a wagon with some other kids. We were all taken to live at Mistress Sheba's farm.'

Dayton would have liked to question her further about her home, but Debbie was only four. She couldn't have known what towns she had passed through, or even what state or territory.

'Do you know the man who took you?' he asked.

'It was Mr Collinsworth,' she answered. 'We slept in the wagon and he fed us hard rolls and jerky. We were in the wagon a long time before we got to the farm.'

Dayton reasoned that Larkin likely had a standing order for children. Debbie and those others were likely from somewhere within California.

'Get some sleep, Squirt,' he said softly. 'I won't let anyone take you away. I promise.'

'Will you stay here next to me until I go to sleep?'

Resigning himself to losing another few minutes of his own sleep, Dayton told her he would and hunkered down by her bed. Debbie took his hand, coddled it next to her cheek and closed her eyes. Dayton whispered to her softly, telling her she was safe and how she was going to be happy again. It took but a short while before Debbie's breathing grew steady and he carefully removed his hand. Then he crept over to his bed and began to move his things to the floor.

8

'Who are you?' Molly's excited voice came from downstairs. 'What are you doing in my house?'

Dayton had not yet got into bed. He grabbed his gun, bolted from the room and scrambled down the stairway. He reached the bottom floor just as Molly cried out. From the dim flicker of the always lit entrance-way lamp, he saw that a shadowy figure had knocked Molly aside and was making a dash for the front door.

'Hold it!' Dayton shouted. 'Stop, or I'll shoot!'

The figure spun about and a flash of light and gun blast exploded from the muzzle of a pistol. The bullet slapped into the wall next to Dayton and he instantly returned fire. Worried that Molly could get hit if the man got off another shot, he sent round after round at the shooter. He stopped pulling the trigger when he had spent all but his last bullet; then he stood, crouched and ready, watching the phantom's movements.

It was bizarre, but the man remained standing near the door. His weapon dropped noisily to the floor, lying harmless at his feet, yet he didn't move. Dayton kept his gun pointed at the intruder and moved towards him. Molly had remained on the floor, but she had crawled into one of the vacant rooms. She peered out, while still on her hands and knees.

'You get him?' She whispered the question.

Dayton didn't reply until he reached the dark figure. He discovered the man was pinned against the counter. The coat hanger from the wall had hooked the collar of his jacket and kept him upright. His arms hung limply at his side, his mouth agape and eyes fixed and staring. He was dead.

'Bless my bunions!' Molly exclaimed,

having followed along behind Dayton. 'It's Mr Gant!'

Dayton saw some papers sticking out of his jacket. He turned up the lamp and removed them.

'He has my list of names from the state,' he advised Molly.

'I heard the moving around and decided to talk to you about the children.' She explained how she had come upon the intruder. 'When I got to the door, Gant had a knife in one hand and was going through your room. The blankets were bunched on your bed and I thought he might have killed you.'

'I'm sure that was his plan.'

Molly frowned. 'Where were you?'

He explained how Debbie's nightmare had probably saved his life. Then he said, 'Better go up and let the children know everything is all right. The shooting will have woken the whole house. I'm going to get the sheriff and bring him over here. I want to get this cleared up tonight. Come morning, I'm going to ride out to

Larkin's place and do some looking around.'

'You go there alone and you'll be killed!'

'I'll take the sheriff.'

Molly laughed at the notion. 'The sheriff would most likely shoot you in the back.'

'Then I'll make other arrangements,' Dayton said. 'One way or the other, I'll get to the bottom of this.'

'Salty told me another man arrived from Shilo today. He didn't know who he was, but he sent a telegraph message to Shilo and let the sheriff there know he had arrived. He was going to meet up with some bounty hunters who are searching for Alyson.'

'If my brother is doing his job, the bounty on Alyson should be withdrawn shortly. I'll deliver her for a new trial or she will be acquitted outright.'

Molly gave him a puzzled look. 'You have a rather high opinion of your brother if you think he can get a murder charge dropped after a person has been sentenced.'

Dayton grinned. 'It isn't what he can do, Molly. I've a few influential friends of my own.'

She grunted, as if all was lost. 'I feared as much when you first told me what you had in mind . . . you're plumb loco!'

★   ★   ★

Deputy Hancock was the one sleeping at the jail. He was none too happy about being forced to wake up the sheriff in the middle of the night.

Byers also displayed irritation for the interruption to his slumber. He grumbled and cursed profanely as he dressed. Once he had joined them he frowned at Hancock.

'I don't see what could be so all-fired important that it couldn't wait until morning.'

'Don't bite my head off, Sheriff. This is all on Garrett here. He said we had to come now.'

Dayton didn't fill them in until they reached the boarding house. Byers's mutterings ceased when he saw a dead man standing vertical at the counter.

'What the hell?' he bellowed.

'Keep your voice down,' Dayton scolded him. 'Molly is trying to get the kids back to sleep. Made one heck of a loud racket, this guy and me throwing lead at each other.'

'It's Fillmore Gant!' Byers declared. 'What's he doing here?'

'He came to kill me in my sleep and steal the records about the children Larkin is using for his slave labor.'

The name of Larkin abruptly altered Byers's stance. 'You ain't suggesting that Larkin had anything to do with this?'

Dayton fixed an icy stare at the man. 'Why else would Gant try to kill me? Why steal the records I brought with me from the state agency? Gant is Larkin's hired killer. He wouldn't have done this on his own.'

Byers's jaw became anchored with

defiance. 'Look here, Mr state agency man. I'm not about to ride out and accuse Mr Larkin of sending a killer after you. He pays our wages.' He gave a snort of contempt. 'Besides which, he controls most of the town. It's his money and hired men who support 'most everything around here.'

Molly had come down to tell her part of the attack. She heard the sheriff's comments and strode smartly up to confront him.

'That miserable sneak in the night come into my boarding house,' she said hotly. 'He entered Dayton's room to kill him and steal his papers. The filthy scoundrel knocked me down and might have killed me too, except Dayton come down the stairs and scared him off. When he shouted at Gant to stop, the man turned and fired his gun at Dayton. That was a stupid mistake on his part, because Dayton was on the dark stairway while Gant was outlined by the night lamp. There's no question about this intrusion or the man's mission. Now, either you do your job, Sheriff, or I'll personally start a campaign to remove you from office.'

Byers snickered. 'Who do you think you are, Molly? You ain't got the sand nor the backing to have me replaced.'

'You're wrong on both counts,' Dayton announced.

Before Byers or Hancock could react, Dayton drew his gun and covered the pair.

'Stand still or I'll plug you both!' he threatened. Turning his head to the side, but keeping his eyes on the duo, he spoke to Molly. 'Go get Sarge. I'm appointing him temporary sheriff of Larkinville.'

Molly's eyes were wide with surprise. She gazed down at Dayton's gun and then stared at him.

'Are you sure about this?' she asked nervously. 'I mean, can you do this?'

'Trust me,' Dayton retorted easily. 'Get the sergeant.'

★ ★ ★

Dayton and Sarge were at the jail the next morning when a rider dismounted at the hitching rail. Spotting the man through the building's only window, Dayton asked Byers if he knew him. Byers looked through the bars and grunted.

'It's that German from Shilo,' he said. 'He's a Bismark and he is going to join up with the bounty hunter, Rico Santana, and his two Indian trackers. They are searching for the female prisoner who escaped the other night.'

Dayton tipped his head to Sarge, indicating he should speak to the man. Rather than allow the stranger to enter, Nolan went out on to the step to meet him.

'What the devil?' the man exclaimed, seeing Nolan's badge. 'What happened to the other sheriff? I just talked to him last night.'

'Caught him dealing off the bottom of the deck at the casino,' Nolan said simply. 'We don't tolerate any manner of crookedness in this here town. I'm the new sheriff. What can I do for you?'

'The name is Wolfgang Bismark,' the guy replied. 'I just wanted to let someone know where I would be and how to contact me if any telegraph messages should come in.'

'You're staying at the hotel?'

'That's right.'

'All right. If any messages come in for you, I'll have Salty send them over there. You can check whenever you are in town that way.'

Wolfgang stood for a long moment, peering into the dark interior of the jail.

'Cheating at cards, huh?' He chuckled. 'Man, you people run a puritanical little town.'

'Can't have a sinner wearing a badge,' Nolan stated. 'Anything else I can do for you?'

'You might keep an eye out for a handsome lady with long, red-gold hair. She's wanted for murder in Shilo. If you catch her, there's a two-hundred-dollar reward.'

'I'll keep an eye peeled,' Sarge promised.

Wolfgang lifted a hand in departure and mounted his horse. Then he neck-reined the animal around and headed out of town.

Nolan returned inside the office and paused to take a sip of his medicine before he closed the door. Dayton had overheard the conversation and moved up next to him.

'So that's one of the Bismark family?'

'Wolfgang,' Nolan said, returning the flask to his back pocket. 'I heard from a passing freighter that he's got a bad temper and has beaten up more than one of the Bismark teamsters.'

'And he is joining in the hunt for Alyson,' Dayton mused. 'That's just what we needed.'

'Mind telling me how you intend for us to handle Larkin?' Nolan eyed him curiously. 'I mean, the man still has two or three gunhands and a host of people working for him. Hard to say how many of them will take up arms against us.'

'You saw the condition of those kids,' Dayton said. 'Little Debbie has blisters on her feet from trying to work in shoes that didn't fit right. Rather than treat her sore feet and get her proper-fitting footwear, they were going to get rid of her. According to Matthew, once a child is sent to the house, they are never seen or heard from again.'

'Damn,' Nolan said softly. 'Can you imagine, letting that beautiful little girl starve or die from tainted water or food? And all because she isn't big enough to do a good day's work.'

'I've got to put a stop to it, Sarge.'

'But how?' Nolan wanted to know. 'I'm not sure how much of a posse we can gather. I suspect there's a good many men around here who would be on Larkin's side rather than against him.'

'Matthew told me about the men out at the farm. Fillmore Gant was the worst, and he's being fitted for a box.' Dayton held up three fingers. 'That leaves the children's overseer, Seeton, who, Matthew thinks, is ignorant about the killing of children; Collinsworth, who is a back-shooter and second in command; and finally Jammer, the brute with the dogs. I figure two or three men ought to be enough to get the job done.'

'What about the sher . . . uh,' he caught himself before he called Byers the sheriff, 'I mean, our two prisoners?'

'I'm going to make them a proposition they can't refuse,' Dayton said. 'They will either take the offer or it'll be too bad for both of them.'

⋆　⋆　⋆

Collinsworth entered the Larkin house and found Sheba and Walt at the breakfast table. He removed his hat, as if attending a funeral, and approached the pair.

'Well?' Sheba demanded at once. 'Where is Gant? Why hasn't he reported in?'

'Gant's laid out at the carpenter's

place, deader'n your shoe leather,' Collinsworth answered. 'He traded shots with that agency fellow and got a bellyful of lead.'

'What?' Walt cried. 'Gant wasn't supposed to get into a gunfight.'

'That isn't all,' Collinsworth continued. 'Byers and Hancock are in jail.'

'You mean *at* the jail, don't you?' Sheba corrected.

'No, ma'am,' Collinsworth said. 'The retired solider, who lives at Widow Dexter's boarding house, is now wearing the star. He locked them both up.'

Walt was too dumbstruck to speak. Sheba swore and rose to her feet, a seething rage turning her face bright red. 'This can't be happening!' she howled. 'Walt!' She turned on her husband. 'On whose authority can they do that?'

'It was the state agency fellow who done arrested Byers and Hancock,' Collinsworth clarified. 'He appointed old Jack Nolan as the new sheriff.'

'What gives that jackal so much

clout?' Walt huffed with exasperation. 'He's only an official for the state child service.'

'Right or wrong, with or without authority, boss, them two are sitting in a cell and Nolan is wearing the star.'

Sheba began to pace the room. 'No one in their right mind would appoint that old army sergeant to be sheriff. Rumor has it he is dying. The agent must have some kind of plan.'

'Maybe he's going to have an election for sheriff?' Walt suggested.

'Everyone knows Gant worked for you.' Collinsworth stated the obvious. 'What if Garrett comes riding out here with a posse?'

Walt grunted his disdain. 'Who would he get to side him against us?'

Sheba picked up her quirt, still prowling like a cornered cat. 'We can't underestimate him a second time,' she said. 'He took Gant in a gun battle. Now he's arrested our sheriff and deputy and locked them up. He wouldn't have taken such drastic steps unless he thought he could back them up.'

Walt didn't argue with his wife. Rather, he let her continue pondering the situation. In times of stress, and once her initial rage was under control, she was the brains behind their modest empire.

'We need someone outside for a job like this,' she said after a short span of time, 'a hired killer who can get rid of this pest once and for all.'

'If you want to spend the money,' Collinsworth suggested. 'Savage Rodriguez holds up at a place over near San Bernardino. He rides with a couple of tough *hombres* and hires out to the highest bidder. Gant told me he was one of the best at making problems go away.'

Sheba didn't hesitate. 'Get him here as quickly as possible.'

Collinsworth didn't bother checking with Walt. He knew the chain of command. Whirling about, he left the room and went out of the house.

'What if Rodriguez doesn't get here in time?' Walt asked once he and Sheba were alone.

Sheba was already thinking along those lines. 'Tell Jammer to stick by the house and keep the dogs handy. If that snoopy agent shows up, he is to stop him . . . using any amount of force necessary.'

'I'll have Seeton move the children to the lower fields. That way, Garrett won't be able to talk to them without us knowing about it.'

'Good thinking.' Sheba approved of the idea. 'What about Byers and Hancock? Will they keep their mouths shut?'

Walt snorted. 'They know what'll happen if they don't.'

Sheba slammed her quirt down on the tabletop. 'I don't know who Dayton Garrett thinks he is,' she hissed the words through her clenched teeth, 'but we will teach him not to mess with us!'

★ ★ ★

Ludwig waited until Erich arrived at his desk, then he forked over a piece of paper.

'Knute brought this by. He wanted me to know about it, because he didn't wish to go behind our backs. It's a telegraph message he wired to the President.'

'President?' Erich repeated, looking at the paper. 'You mean *the* President?'

'None other. It's a request that he intervene on Alyson's behalf and demand a hearing by an impartial judge.'

Erich's head swiveled back and forth as he attempted to comprehend the implication. When he managed speech his voice held a degree of awe.

'That's incredible, Pa. What makes Knute think the President would listen to a small-town attorney like him?'

'Look at the way he signed the message.'

'Knute and Dayton Garrett.' Erich frowned. 'Knute is using his brother's influence? How does his brother have any influence with the President?'

'I asked Knute once about his family. He has a mother who lives a couple hours away and a brother he hasn't seen in years. When he spoke of Dayton, he said he had worked at a number of important jobs including one for the Treasury Department. I'm guessing that's where the influence comes from. His brother must have done something that earned him the thanks of the President.'

'And Knute decided to collect on that debt.'

It was a statement but Ludwig answered: 'So it seems.'

'The governor won't ignore an order from the President. What are you going to do?'

His father rubbed his temples as if he had a throbbing headache. After a few seconds he rose slowly from his desk and paced around the room. He stopped to look through his office window, with his back to Erich, before he eventually broke the silence.

'I know you were never in favor of hanging Alyson,' he said. 'She has escaped twice, but Rico and Wolfgang are on her trail. When they catch her — '

Erich deduced where this was going. 'You don't mean they are going to kill her?'

'Wolfgang volunteered to help bring her back,' Ludwig replied. He turned around to look at his son and his shoulders gave a helpless shrug. 'I don't think we can expect the girl to be alive by the time Wolfgang and Rico arrive.'

'You have to stop them! If this comes to an investigation, we will be the ones to end up behind bars. No honest jury would have found Alyson guilty of murder. Hans had roughed up too many women; too many people know the kind of man he was. You let those men kill her and you might be the one who ends up on the gallows.'

'You want me to just forget about your brother?'

'Hans was fun to be around when it

was just us boys, Pa, but he was an animal when there was a woman or girl about. Hell, he tried to force his attentions on the Lindsey girl when we lived next to them — and she was only twelve years old.'

'That proves nothing.' Ludwig defended his son. 'Hans was only three or four years older than her at the time. It was a boyish prank.'

'You can fool yourself all you want, Pa,' Erich maintained. 'If it comes to an honest-to-goodness trial Knute will find people to testify about Hans. You won't be able to hide the truth.'

'What are you proposing, son? That we let the woman get away with murder?'

Erich sighed. 'We both know it was self-defense and an accident.'

'Then you believe I should try and call off Wolfgang and Rico; let the girl remain a fugitive from the law.'

'It's about the only punishment you can hope for,' Erich said. 'Without a new trial or governor's pardon, she might keep hiding from the law and running.'

Ludwig was torn with regret, remorse and guilt. He should have reined in Hans. Maybe if he had beaten him with a horsewhip for touching the first girl, or allowed him be charged with the physical attack the next time it happened — possibly let him spend a little time in prison? Maybe something would have gotten through his thick head so he wouldn't act like a young bull around a pen full of heifers in season. He should have done a lot of things, but he had looked the other way, pretended the aggressive behavior wasn't that serious. He had failed to act. Now his boy was dead and he was trying to execute a young woman for defending herself. He'd been angry, hurt . . . and wrong.

'All right, Erich.' He gave in. 'Contact Rico and Wolfgang. Tell them to let the girl alone. We'll pay Rico what we promised and Wolfgang can come on home. I'll speak to the judge and you can visit Knute and advise him that we've decided to reverse the court's decision and grant a pardon to Alyson.'

Erich's shoulders became erect and his chin lifted with a trace of pride.

'I'll tell Knute and then send off the telegram.' He started to back away, then paused and said, 'It's the right thing to do, Father. I know it's hard for you, but it will make our position in the town that much stronger.'

'Yes, son,' Ludwig allowed. 'I'm sure you're right.'

Even as Erich hurried from his office, Ludwig battled the sting of tears in his eyes. He had used his anger and desire for retribution to stave off the true loss of his son. Now he was both imbued with the weight of that loss and forced to accept the truth about his boy.

9

Dayton had given the ex-sheriff and deputy an ultimatum. He was lounging in front of the jail, giving the two men time to stew on the idea for a few minutes, when the runner from the telegraph office arrived. It was Salty's oldest boy and he looked excited.

'This just arrived from Shilo,' he said, panting from the short but hard run. 'Pa said to get it right to you.'

Dayton took the paper, removed a two-bit piece from his pocket and handed it to the boy. The kid's eyes lit up and a grin spread across his face so broad it nearly touched his ears on either side. He shouted, 'Thanks a lot!' and raced back to the general store.

'What's it say?' Nolan had come up behind him and was standing in the doorway.

An odd combination of regret and

satisfaction shot through Dayton. It was good news for Alyson, yet it meant she might no longer need his protection. What would he do or say if she decided to simply take the two kids and leave? There was something very special about Alyson, and Dayton could not deny the attraction he felt for her.

'One of our problems is solved,' Dayton finally replied. 'At least, the problem of Alyson being wanted by the law.'

'That's good news.'

'Only if Wolfgang and the bounty hunters are willing to give up their pursuit. Alyson said the Bismark family would hunt her down regardless of any ruling by a judge.'

Nolan snorted. 'Guess that means you and I will have to explain it to them.'

Dayton grinned. 'Don't be in such an all-fired hurry to get yourself killed. We'll see how this plays out after Wolfgang gets his telegram.'

Nolan laughed. 'Well, sure, Garrett.

That's kind of what I meant.'

'What about some help if we have to move against the Larkin place?'

The question sobered the new sheriff. 'I've got the young man who often rides guard on the stage, Rowdy Booth, plus a wandering gambler who goes by the name of Frenchy, and a crippled ex-soldier I've had a few drinks with — Hammer Lockwood. Ain't much of a posse, but 'most everyone else in the valley is scared of offending the Larkins.'

'Five of us ought to be enough.'

'Give the word when you need us and we'll be ready,' Nolan vowed.

Dayton bobbed his head in appreciation. 'I'm going out there tonight to try to get the proof we need. If I find what I'm looking for, we'll hit Larkin before he can put another plan in place.'

'What'll we do till dark?'

Garrett said, 'Come with me,' and entered the jail. Byers and Hancock stood up, both of them gripping the steel bars, anxious and none too happy about their situation.

'What'll it be, boys?' Dayton asked. 'When I arrest Larkin, you two will be charged as his accomplices. Even if you claim innocence about killing off several of the children, you will probably end up serving five to ten years in prison.'

Byers looked as if someone had sucker-punched him in the gut.

'Killing children?' He shook his head. 'We don't know nuthen' about killing any children.'

'I'll have the proof soon enough. Larkin and his wife will be sitting in the cell next to you boys by sometime tomorrow.'

Byers exchanged looks with Hancock. 'We always had a hankering to go ride up to Santa Fe. There's some big cattle ranches getting started over that way.'

'One hour,' Dayton warned them. 'You leave within the hour and never return. If you try and warn the Larkins or show up in California again, there will be warrants issued for your arrest.'

Less than thirty minutes later the two men left by the north trail and were quickly out of sight. With the jail empty, Nolan took Dayton around and introduced him to the three posse members. Each of them showed concern about a child-slavery ring and none were worried about repercussions from the townsfolk. Dayton thanked them for their courage and promised to try and limit any violence when it came time to make arrests.

As he and Nolan were arranging to have horses ready for the next day — two of the men didn't own a horse — several riders appeared, coming down the street. It was Wolfgang and the bounty hunters.

'Trouble,' Nolan said under his breath.

The four men arrived and stopped their mounts a few feet away. Wolfgang eyed them with a curious and mildly suspicious look.

'I found Rico here less than a mile out of town,' he said. 'They finally located that elusive trail.'

'There's a telegraph message at the hotel for you,' Dayton informed the man. 'We got one at the sheriff's office too. The charges against the gal you're looking for have been dismissed and the guilty verdict was overturned.'

'That so?' Wolfgang's expression didn't change. 'Makes no never-mind to us. We are taking her back regardless of what any judge or even the governor might say.'

'If the woman shows up here,' Nolan stated firmly, 'she can expect the protection of the law. I won't stand for anyone trying to harm or abduct a law-abiding citizen on account of a personal vendetta.'

Wolfgang sneered, 'You're a sight too old to be letting your mouth run away with your good sense, Sheriff.'

'The sheriff has my support in this matter,' Dayton responded to the threat.

Rico leaned over the pommel of his saddle and spoke up. 'The tracks we found lead back to town, mister, and we don't believe the rider was the woman. Someone with a lot of tracking knowledge made that escape trail.'

Dayton gave a bob of his head. 'If you're right, that means your fugitive must have gone in a different direction. I reckon she is out of the country by this time.'

Wolfgang said, 'Either that, or she's still close by and someone is hiding her.'

'Feel free to look around,' Nolan offered. 'But remember what I said. You try taking anyone with you by force and you will end up behind bars.'

Without another word the four riders turned their horses for the nearest saloon.

'Seems we've still got the same number of problems as before,' Nolan said to Dayton. 'Betcha we're going to have to deal with those jaspers before we are rid of them.'

'You keep an eye on them. I was going to send off a telegram anyway. I'll let my brother know about Wolfgang. He may be able to offer some help with him and the bounty hunters.'

'I hope so, Garrett, 'cause we've already got our hands full with the Larkins.'

*   *   *

Knute strode into the sheriff's office and planted himself in front of Erich's desk. He had a telegraph message in his hand.

'This just arrived from Larkinville. Your cousin is refusing to call off the hunt for Alyson Walsh,' he told Erich. 'He claims he and those bounty hunters won't quit until they catch her. I believe he intends to kill the woman.'

Erich narrowed his gaze. 'How did you get this information so fast? I only sent the telegram to Wolfgang a few hours ago.'

'My brother is in Larkinville. He's working a child custody case for the state's attorney.'

'And he also just happened to run into Wolfgang?'

'Actually, he is working with the local sheriff. It was the sheriff who told him about your cousin.'

A light of understanding glimmered within Erich's eyes. 'And was this brother of yours here in town the night Alyson broke jail?'

Knute didn't want to lie to Erich, but he couldn't turn in his own brother for a rescue he had inspired him to undertake. Instead of answering the question, he altered his approach.

'You were the only one of your family who didn't want Alyson hanged. I trust that you have the highest moral conscience of the entire Bismark family. It's the reason your father made you sheriff, even though Otto is the eldest boy in the family.'

'You have a fancy way of dancing around a question,' Erich replied. 'It's easy to see why you are a lawyer.'

'What are you going to do about Wolfgang?' Knute kept to his purpose.

'If he goes up against my brother, one of us will lose a relative . . . and it will likely be you.'

'Pa told me about your brother. He's what — kind of a traveling trouble-shooter or something?'

'He has been involved in a good many conflicts, beginning with the war. Dee is not like the passive or easily intimidated men your cousin targets here in town. If Wolfgang pushes him, he will wind up buried next to Hans.' Knute had raised his voice with the impassioned declaration. He calmed himself at once and held out his hand in a soliciting gesture.

'Look, Erich, I'm not trying to bully you into doing what's right. I don't use Wolfgang's tactics. I'm only trying to ensure that justice is done for Alyson Walsh, and I don't wish anyone else to be harmed or killed. That includes Wolfgang and my brother.'

'I'll talk to my father and Uncle Klaus. If nothing else can stop Wolfgang, I'll ride up to Larkinville myself and take charge of the situation. Will that suit you?'

'Absolutely, Sheriff.' Knute was intentionally respectful. 'As I've already expressed, I've always admired your high moral character. I know you'll do what is right.'

Erich grinned, but displayed no humor. 'Your brother is the one who broke Alyson out of my jail. I'm not sure how to deal with that.'

'I have no knowledge of the event, Sheriff.' Knute maintained his aplomb. 'He indicated that he met the girl on the trail and she duped him with a story and stole his horse.'

'And she just happened to be on her way to Larkinville,' Erich finished wryly. 'Then she also happened to bust out of their jail. Now your brother seems to know where she is and is trying to save her from Wolfgang and the bounty hunters.'

Knute did not respond to the assumptions. 'Thank you again, Sheriff. I hope this can be resolved quickly, before anyone gets hurt.'

'Yeah, right, Lawyer Garrett. I'll get right on it.'

* * *

Dayton tried to take an afternoon nap, knowing he would be out for most of the night. He had settled down on his bunk, hat tipped over his eyes, when he felt someone next to him. He lifted up his hat and saw Debbie. She displayed a timorous simper, climbed up on to the bed and curled up under his left arm.

'You have a bed if you're tired,' he said softly.

'Uh-huh,' she acknowledged, as she put her hands under her head and snuggled up against him.

With a sigh of defeat, Dayton lowered his arm to encircle her shoulders. It was all the encouragement the child needed. She exchanged the makeshift pillow of her own two hands and placed her cheek on the crook of his arm. Within a few minutes she was asleep. Dayton was stuck, having to remain in that position, but he did manage to doze for a few minutes. Even that was interrupted a short while later when Alyson entered the room.

'Oh!' she said, causing Debbie to awaken. 'I'm sorry, Dayton. I was afraid Debbie had gone off on her own somewhere. I've been looking all over for her.'

Debbie sat up and stretched. Dayton grimaced as he found himself able to move his arm for the first time in an hour. Alyson smiled at his discomfort, laughing silently with her eyes.

'I should have known she was with you.'

'She needs a nap now and again until she regains her strength.' Dayton made her excuse. 'And she needs to add a few pounds.'

'Sarge told me about the warrant for me being withdrawn. Is it true? Did the Bismarks actually overturn my conviction?'

'That's what the telegraph message

said.' He remained serious. 'However, Wolfgang is not going to honor the verdict. He still intends to hunt you down.'

'What should I do?'

'For the time being, stick with the plan. If no one recognizes you, I'll sort this out once I get everything straight with the Larkins.'

'Sarge told me you are going out to their place tonight to snoop around. What do you hope to accomplish?'

'According to Matthew, the overseer named Seeton keeps a daily record of the kids' work. That could be the evidence I need to place the Larkins under arrest and start a search.'

'You mean for the missing . . . '

A sharp look from Dayton stopped her from finishing the sentence. Debbie didn't appear to be listening closely, but she was still in the room.

'Debbie, honey,' Alyson spoke to the child, 'why don't you go wash up for dinner. Then you can go and see if Molly needs you to help set the table.'

The little waif said a cheerful, 'OK', and hurried from the room. Alyson waited until she was through the door before she approached Dayton. When she was a step away, he gazed into her inviting eyes.

'This sounds like a dangerous idea,' she began, speaking softly. 'What if you are caught?'

Dayton got to his feet before answering. 'I've often traveled through Indian territory, missy. I know how to use the darkness to cover my movements. I'll be all right.'

Alyson revealed the same hesitation he had seen before, the parting of her lips, words halted at the last possible moment, yet her intentions were clandestinely communicated by the subtle desire in her rich green eyes. Dayton had missed his chance the last time she had approached him; he didn't make the same mistake again. Reaching out, he placed his hands on Alyson's shoulders and gently coerced her to move a step closer. Her body yielded willingly to his touch. He encircled her within his arms, leaned down and kissed her.

Alyson allowed the intimate liberty, naively awkward, yet moderately receptive. Dayton didn't linger, but tightened his embrace and placed his cheek against her own.

'You're the only woman I will ever want in my life, Alyson,' he whispered in her ear. 'I've never been in love, but I'm pretty certain I'm in love with you.'

Alyson drew back enough so that she could look up at him, scrutinizing, searching for something in his adoring eyes. Then her long lashes lowered with the shutting of her eyes and her lips found his. There was no indecision this second time. She kissed him back.

★   ★   ★

According to Matthew, Seeton was somewhat childlike and slept in the large bunkhouse with the children. He supposedly had his own room, stationed at the main exit where he could keep watch on any goings or comings. Matt also said Seeton was friendly, gentle and never raised his voice, which made him the perfect supervisor to offset the volatile Mistress Sheba.

Dayton picketed his horse a half-mile from the plantation buildings and made his approach after full dark, crossing through several acres of potatoes. The bushy tops of the plants only reached his ankles, but he could drop to his belly and be completely out of sight in an instant. His big concern was not for a night guard, but that they might have the dogs prowling the grounds. No amount of hiding would keep a hound from picking up his scent.

The lights at the main house remained on after both the bunkhouses were dark. Dayton used those lights to keep his bearings, and reached a point where he could view the yard. It took patience before he finally spotted a dog at each entrance to the big house. Obviously, Walt and Sheba's primary concern was their own security. The positive side was that the dogs were tethered on a length of rope and secured at a stake next to the building. They had a range of only about thirty feet.

Moving slowly and keeping low, Dayton put the Yard House between him and the watchdogs. Then he crept forward to the side of the building. The windows on the upper floor were open several inches, but not the ones on the ground floor. That was probably to keep any of the kids from being able to slip out during the night.

Dayton's heart began to pound as he ventured around the corner of the building. If one of the dogs spotted him he would be in for the fight of his life. Also, this had to be done covertly if it were to work. It forced him to move only a few inches at a time, all the while hoping the dogs did not see him. Luckily, a slight breeze wafted across his face, so he was downwind of the animals.

Sweat beaded his brow and dampened spots under his arms from the strain. He finally reached the door and tested it. Thankfully, it was not bolted from the inside. Dayton slipped inside the gloomy interior of the bunkhouse and eased the door closed behind him. Then he remained motionless for a few moments and listened intently while his eyes adjusted to the darkness. Seeton's room had a door, while the rest of the place was nothing but rows of bunks, with single storage boxes for possessions at the foot of the bedsteads.

Dayton stepped gingerly over to the door, pushed it open and eased quietly into Seeton's room. The man stirred and sat up as he reclosed the door.

'Who is it?' Seeton muttered. 'Can't this wait until morning?'

Dayton struck a match and raised his other hand, with the palm outward in a calming gesture.

'Sorry to wake you, Mr Seeton,' he

said quietly. 'I only need a moment of your time.'

'I know you,' Seeton said. 'You're the guy who took some of the kids away.'

'Yes,' Dayton replied, lighting the lamp and turning the wick up enough to illuminate the room. 'Matthew said you were the man in charge of the children.'

Seeton swung his bare feet over the edge of his bunk. 'Yeah, I watch over the kids,' he agreed. 'It's my job. I do a good job too. You can ask anyone.'

Dayton smiled, taking a seat on a chair next to a tiny desk. 'This where you do all of your record-keeping?'

Seeton flashed a simpleton's grin. 'Yeah. I make a weekly copy for Mistress Sheba every Saturday night. She says I do real good.' His chest puffed up. 'Mistress counts on me to see that everyone is doing their jobs.'

Dayton realized that Matt had been on point. Seeton was immature in many ways, seeking approval and doing what he was told. He used that approach.

'Matthew told me you kept the best records of anyone he ever knew. Can you tell me about it?'

'What for?' Seeton asked. 'I thought you took the only kids whose parents had come looking for them.'

'Yes, that's right, Mr Seeton, but your records might lead me to a couple more.' As the man frowned in apparent ignorance he went on: 'You see, there were six names missing from the list, six kids who came here within the last two years but are no longer on the farm. I thought your record-keeping might be able to pinpoint the exact dates each of them left.'

'Well, yeah,' Seeton replied with confidence. 'I make an entry in my log for each worker every single day. When one of them don't show up, I make a note of it. Mistress Sheba is very strict that I keep exact records.'

'Can you show me the dates when each of those kids stopped showing up for work and maybe tell me the reason?' Dayton enquired. 'That would allow me to know where to start looking.'

'I can show you in the book, but each and every one of them went to the hospital,' Seeton said. 'When one of the workers gets sick or hurt, they stay here in the Yard House a day or two. If they don't get better, Mistress Sheba takes them into the main house. If they still don't get well, she has them taken to the hospital.'

'Have you ever been to the hospital? Do you know where it is?'

'I ain't never been sick enough to have to go,' Seeton explained. 'I asked Collinsworth about it one time and he said it was a long way off.'

'Well, I'm sure I can find it,' Dayton said. 'If you show me the records for the six children, I'll be able to locate them and maybe get them home to their families.'

'Yeah.' Seeton bobbed his head. 'I'll be glad to help with that. Let me put on my pants and I'll find you the right pages. I date every one, so you can see when they came down sick and the very day each of them went to the hospital.'

'Sheba is right,' Dayton praised. 'You are the right man for this job.'

★   ★   ★

Erich pushed open the door to Wolfgang's room and posed with his hands on his hips, glaring at his sleepy-eyed cousin. The man had evidently been drinking most of the night, as he stared back with red-rimmed eyes and a haggard, pale face.

'What's the deal here, Cuz?' Erich demanded to know. 'You were to call off Rico and return to Shilo.'

Wolfgang recovered his wits and sneered back. 'You don't run me, Erich. You can walk tall and flash your badge around Shilo, but you're sixty miles out of your jurisdiction.'

'Klaus wants you home, before you do something stupid . . . like killing a woman who has been declared innocent in the death of Hans.'

'And you're going along with that,

huh?' Wolfgang snorted his contempt. 'You always were the high-minded Christian sort in the family, spouting about love and forgiveness. Well, that don't wash with me. I'm more Old Testament — an eye for an eye!'

'I spoke to the sheriff here and he said he warned you not to try and kidnap anyone from his town. My father and yours are telling you the same thing. We don't want any more blood over Hans's death.'

Wolfgang didn't budge. 'I'll head back when I'm good and ready, Erich. If you stick around here I might have to show you who is the better man.'

'I didn't come here for a fight,' Erich replied. 'I came here to stop you from having your name end up on a Wanted poster. If you kill Alyson there will be no protecting you. I would hate to be the one to arrest you for her murder.'

'G'wan home, Erich.' Wolfgang ended the conversation. He lay back down and pulled the blanket over his head. 'I'm gonna finish what we started.'

Erich fumed silently, then turned around and left the room. He had expected resistance from his cousin, but not a complete dismissal. Ludwig's order and the support of Wolfgang's own father meant nothing. Hans and Wolfgang had been close growing up, Wolfgang's closest friend or relative. The man meant to have his pound of flesh, even if it meant going to prison.

Pausing at the hotel entrance, Eric looked up and down the street and suddenly had a thought. Why was his cousin still in Larkinville? How did Rico and Wolfgang intend to find the girl? They had gotten drunk the previous night and were sleeping late. That didn't seem to be the best use of time when chasing after someone who could be a hundred miles away by now. Unless . . . ?

'They think the girl is here,' he deduced aloud.

10

The Sarge gathered the three volunteers and brought them to the sheriff's office. Dayton explained what he had found.

'Seeton keeps impeccable records,' he told the group. 'Every child who came to work was included in his daily logs. He recorded the amount of work each one did every day for Mrs Larkin and never missed an entry. I have the dates each of the six missing children arrived and the day they went missing. Seeton was told those children were too ill or injured to work and had been taken to a hospital. I believe the truth is much more sinister.'

'And if we find some bodies, the Larkins will end up in prison,' Rowdy declared.

'Or hanged,' Dayton replied. 'They either allowed those children to die or they helped them along with a little poison or something. From what I saw, Walt and Sheba Larkin do not have a lot of compassion or patience.'

'Let's ride out and see what we can find,' Frenchy suggested. 'If what you suspect is true, these inhuman savages must pay for the lives they have stolen.'

'I agree,' Lockwood joined in.

'Hold it.' Nolan quieted the group. 'We've got company.'

Erich Bismark appeared at the doorway and lifted his brows in surprise.

'What's this? A posse of some kind?'

'What can we do for you?' Dayton asked him.

'I spoke to Wolfgang, Garrett. He isn't going to leave.' With a crooked, knowing look he went on, 'I believe he thinks Alyson Walsh is hiding in town or near by.'

Nolan spoke up. 'What does it matter where she is? With the warrant on her revoked, she's no longer wanted by the law.'

'Makes no difference to my cousin.

He's going to cause trouble before this is settled.'

'We have another fish on the line right now,' Dayton informed him. 'I don't suppose you want to tag along?'

'As a spectator or the law?'

'Your sheriff's badge doesn't mean anything here,' Nolan said. 'We are going to visit Larkin's child labor camp and try to find evidence of several missing children. We have to assume they are buried in the grounds.'

Erich's expression darkened. 'You think they have let children die while in their care?'

Dayton answered: 'Records indicate six kids have disappeared over the past sixteen months. All but one of those scored poorly on their daily work record. The sixth was injured by a team of horses and might have died as a result.' Dayton gnashed his teeth. 'None of the deaths were reported or treated by the town's doctor . . . not one.'

'Count me in,' Erich grimly volunteered.

'Glad to have you join us.' Nolan made things official. 'Consider yourself deputized.'

* ★ ★

Facing six men, Jammer kept his dogs on a short leash and did not attempt to oppose the posse. Dayton ignored Sheba and Walt's protests as he gave orders. He had Erich take a couple of men and told him where to dig. Nolan and Frenchy kept watch on the Larkins and forced Jammer to secure the watchdogs. Meanwhile, Dayton took a tour throughout the house and located a small root cellar near the back door.

The dugout had been made into a crude bedroom of sorts, with dirt walls and one grimy little cot on the bare dirt floor. There was a tattered linen sheet, covered in grime, and the single blanket resembled a filthy rag. There was nothing else, other than an empty bucket in one corner. Dayton took a whiff and grimaced. The pail reeked of vomit and human waste. This was the *hospital!*

Picturing a child being stuck in this home-made dungeon caused his stomach to churn and bile to rise in his throat. Dayton scrambled up out of the pit and began to search the house. He didn't have to look long before he espied a jar of peculiar leaves and seeds. Next, he exited the back of the house and checked the small garden area. Not only were there a number of herbs and spice plants, he recognized one rather tall plant with sparse leaf cover and tiny purple flowers. He had heard that particular plant called by several names — fairy bells, fairy finger or fairy caps. But an army post surgeon had told him it was usually called foxglove. It was a form of digitalis, a strong and deadly poison. Tears burned the backs of his eyes as he imagined some poor child being stuck in that dank, dark hole, then given food laced with a poison that would tear their insides apart.

'Garrett!' Rowdy's voice cried out. It

sounded like a mixture of excitement and horror.

Dayton hurried over to the small cleared area that Matthew had indicated. Rowdy and Lockwood both held shovels, but they had stopped digging. Erich was using his hands to clear away the soil. As Dayton approached, he saw a dirt-encrusted burlap sack wrapped around a small form. An exposed hand had slipped between the layers, a small, delicate-looking hand.

'There's more than one,' Erich reported gravely. 'At least three are buried here, and we've barely scraped the surface.'

'Six children on the list of wards assigned to the Larkins are missing,' Dayton said. 'Keep looking and salvage whatever you can. We need to have an army surgeon examine the contents of their stomachs. I'm thinking we'll find the poison these vile monsters used.'

'Doc Brackenbough knows about pharmaceuticals,' Lockwood spoke up. 'He makes most of his own remedies from ordinary herbs and spices.'

'We'll try him first,' Dayton allowed. 'If you think we can trust him.'

'Doc ain't all that fond of Larkin and his wife. He's suspected they were mistreating the kids out here for some time.' Lockwood lifted his shoulders in an understanding shrug. 'He just never had anyone to complain to, what with the law being Larkin's own lackeys.'

'Rowdy,' Dayton instructed, 'get a buckboard for the bodies. Soon as they are recovered, Erich, Sarge and I will take the Larkins to jail and have the doctor check for poison.'

'OK,' the young freighter replied.

'Then, collect all of the kids. You'll need enough transport for the twenty-five children; bring them into town.'

'There are plenty of freight wagons and horses here for the job,' Rowdy said.

'Where are we gonna house that many kids?' Lockwood wanted to know.

'Leave them with Molly at her boarding house. If I'm right about

221

where many of those children came from, she won't have to watch some of them very long.'

'What about the guy with the dogs?' Erich asked.

'We'll take him with us to jail. Matthew said he and Collinsworth were the ones who dug the holes for the bodies.'

Erich understood and asked, 'Speaking of Collinsworth, where is he?'

'I believe he slipped away as we were riding in. My guess is . . . ' Dayton gave a knowing look at Erich, 'he's gone to get help.'

* ★ ★

Wolfgang watched the stage arrive as he was lounging by a window in the saloon. He had given Rico and his Indian pals enough money to buy supplies and get a bottle for their own little party. They would be ready when he'd figured out his next move.

A few minutes after the coach pulled

out the black-haired young woman from the boarding house made her way over to the store. She was inside for a few minutes, then came out with a sack of groceries and a handful of mail. Wolfgang almost dismissed her until she stepped off the walkway. Her skirt lifted up enough for him to see a cream-colored, nicely trim ankle. As she walked toward the boarding house he sat up straight. He had seen that feminine gait before!

Wolfgang studied her from the back. There could be no mistake. Alyson always kept her upper carriage erect and shoulders squared, to reduce any notion of her trying to garner attention. But nature was not so easily dissuaded; the young woman could not control the regular sway of her hips. The skirt gently rocked to one side and then the other with each step. He had admired her form more than once when he and Hans were girl-watching. Oversexed hound that Hans was, he claimed her gait proved the girl wanted attention and was just playing it coy. Wolfgang thought differently. Some women had a natural grace about them, some plodded along like a plow horse, and a few exaggerated their walk to purposely rotate their hips in order to entice a man. Alyson was of the first category.

'So,' he muttered, 'you've been hiding in plain sight.' He gritted his teeth to suppress the boiling fury that invaded his chest. His cousin and lifelong pal was rotting in his grave because of Alyson. He wouldn't rest until she joined him in death. However long he had to wait.

Several riders and a wagon appeared on the main road. Erich was one of them, along with the old sheriff and the state agency man, the one who was looking for missing children. The wagon stopped in front of the doctor's office while the rest of the bunch, including a woman, continued to the jail.

'Didn't think anyone would have the guts,' the barkeep said, having walked over to look out of the window. 'Appears old Sarge arrested the Larkins.' He snorted. 'Bound to be a bloody battle now.'

'How's that?' Wolfgang asked him.

'Larkin has some tough men working for him, and enough money to hire a dozen gunmen. He won't be in jail long, not once his men hear about this. Yep, there's gonna be blood spilt.'

Wolfgang hid a grin of satisfaction. Such a fight sounded like just the kind of diversion he needed.

★　★　★

Soon Jammer and the Larkins were behind bars. Sheba bellowed and screamed all manner of threats, until Sarge doused her with a bucket of water.

'You'll get that every time you open your mouth, unless it's to eat!' he promised her.

Dayton laughed, watching Sheba swear under her breath. 'You make a fair country sheriff.'

Sarge grinned and Dayton left for the boarding house to see about housing twenty-five more kids. Molly and Alyson were busy outlining sleeping arrangements, baths and how to feed so many mouths. Upon his arrival Alyson left Molly to handle the children and hurried over to talk to him.

'You were right!' she exclaimed. 'You were right about everything.'

Dayton was taken back at her exuberance. 'What are you talking about?'

'The children!' she cried. 'Seventeen of them are on that list you requested from Colorado. Seventeen!'

Dayton felt a great wave of relief and satisfaction. 'It makes sense,' he told her. 'The slavers I've been trying to track down dealt with a handful of Indians who kidnapped the children all along the Colorado border. The raiders most often stole the child whenever he or she was alone. The Indian brave I told you about, the wounded warrior, he said they tried not to kill anyone so as to keep the army from coming after them. Kids go missing all the time, getting lost or running away, so most people didn't suspect they were being kidnapped by Indians.'

'Are the Larkins going to tell you who those slavers are and how to find them?'

'So far Sheba has kept a tight rein on the two men. She has vowed we will all be dead in a matter of hours, so they are not talking.'

'What about all of the names that match those on the list?'

'I'll start contacting those parents right away and we will ship the kids off by stagecoach. I'm hopeful we can get most of them out of here before Collinsworth arrives with help. Jammer let slip he had gone to meet a notorious killer named Savage Rodriguez, who was being hired to get rid of me and Sarge.'

'I saw Erich riding with you.' Alyson changed the subject.

'Yes,' Dayton responded. 'He came to take Wolfgang back home, but Wolfgang isn't of a mind to leave without you. Erich signed on to help save the children. He seems a good man.'

'Of all the Bismarks, he is the only one who thought I should not be hanged.'

'When the children arrive, speak to the eight who aren't on the list. See what you can learn about them. Maybe they can think of a relative who might take them in. If not . . . ' Dayton didn't actually know what they would do.

'Molly said she could look after a few, providing the state assigned the wards to her and sent her a little money to help with their upkeep. As an ex-schoolteacher, she would be able to educate the children as well as hire them out for simple jobs around town.'

'I don't know. That would be eleven children,' Dayton said, adding the numbers in his head.

Alyson frowned. 'Eleven? You mean eight.'

'I was counting the two Smith kids and Debbie.'

'You can't give up *our* children!'

Dayton raised his brows in surprise. 'I thought you only wanted to save the kids from the Larkins?'

'Well, yes,' she admitted. 'But with you and me . . . ' She coughed to hide her chagrin. 'I mean, I thought we would look after Ruby and Ken. And,' she added quickly, 'how could you ever tell Debbie you don't want her to be your little girl?'

'I do want her,' Dayton protested. 'But I'm thinking what is best for the children. I don't even have a steady job. I bounce around from place to place and hire out where I can.'

'You can't do that as my husband,' Alyson said sharply. 'I expect to have a home, one with you and me both living and working together.'

'Soon as I clear up this slavery ring, we can decide what we'll do.' He grinned. 'Of course, I've got to survive the attack from Larkin's men first. They may settle the problem for us.'

Alyson surged forward and threw her arms around him. 'Don't even joke about something happening to you,' she murmured. 'I gave you my trust . . . and my love. I've never given either of those to a man before.'

'And I'll do my durndest not to let you down, missy,' he promised, kissing her on the cheek. 'Sarge is going to talk to some of the townsmen and see if we can recruit a little more help. Erich is watching the jail and I've got a man watching the road.' He lifted his head, gazed into Alyson's enchanting eyes and returned to the children. 'For the time being, you help look after the kids and keep an eye out for Wolfgang. I've got to get some men working on a plan I have in mind for dealing with any rescue attempt by Larkin's men. I also need to send off wires to the parents of the children who were stolen from Colorado. Hopefully, we can start shipping some of them home tomorrow.'

Rodriguez didn't get the title of Savage by being subtle, but even he was wary of a couple of lawmen and several members of a posse. Collinsworth gathered three loyal men from the plantation and Rodriguez had four with him. That made a sizeable force, but not enough to take on an entire town.

'Won't be any problem with the locals,' Collinsworth assured him. 'Larkin's money supports 'most every business in town.'

The bunch made their way to the outskirts of Larkinville at dusk. Rodriguez sent one of his men ahead to scout around. He arrived back a few minutes later with his report.

'Seems quiet,' he said. 'Only two men at the jail. Some old guy and one who looks capable.'

'That would be Nolan and Garrett,' Collinsworth surmised. 'They probably don't expect anyone to be coming for Larkin this soon.'

'You saw no one else?' Rodriguez questioned his man. 'No one in the windows, no men with guns standing around?'

'The businesses are mostly closed and the rest of the people are either eating supper or in the saloons drinking and gambling. I didn't see any sentries or guards.'

'This will be the easiest thousand dollars you ever made,' Collinsworth said. 'We kill Nolan and Garrett, bust the Larkins and Jammer out of jail, then pin a badge on another of our own men. Everything will be back to normal.'

With a raising of his hand Rodriguez started the band of men moving. They rode with rifles propped against their thighs, one hand at the stock or barrel, with the guns cocked and ready. They halted at the edge of town, so they could enter two or three at a time. After a few minutes the gang gathered in front of the sheriff's office. Nine rifles pointed at the front of the building when Rodriguez made his demand.

'Give us the Larkins or die!' he shouted. 'You have five seconds before we open fire and take them by force!'

Suddenly, a match flared, then dropped at once into a four-inch-deep trench filled with coal oil. Flames shot up along ditches that ran down either side of the street. Fire lit up the night and ringed the gang of men. The would-be raiders were lit up like actors on a stage, standing in the light of a dozen bright lamps.

'Everybody stay calm!' Dayton's voice boomed. 'There are twenty guns pointed at you!'

Horses danced nervously from the sudden flare-up of fire; saddle leather creaked as men jerked on the reins and twisted about to see through the wall of flames.

Collinsworth looked about wildly and snarled: 'No way they can have that many men. Larkin owns this town.'

'We brought in the bodies of six dead children,' Dayton replied. 'Larkin's money can't buy his way out of this.'

'Children who were poisoned for being too small or too weak to work the fields,' Doc Brackenbough's voice called out. 'God forgive us for not discovering this sooner.'

'And four of us are pointing shotguns at you boys.' Salty added his own threat. 'Any one of you puts up a fight and there won't be enough scraps of meat left for even the buzzards to find.'

From out of the darkness a dozen men appeared, all holding guns. From the porches and roofs of buildings, even more shooters were silhouetted against the night sky.

'Some of you men are not wanted by the law,' Dayton spoke up again. 'You might be able to walk away from this. But if one shot is fired,' he warned, 'we will kill you to the last man.'

Rodriguez swore vehemently. 'We can take them, men,' he shouted. 'Stand with me!'

His frantic order had no effect. Facing such overwhelming odds, the gunmen began tossing down their rifles and raising their hands. Except for Collinsworth and Rodriguez, every single man surrendered without a fight. After a few moments, and confronted by a hopeless situation, the two leaders did the same.

Erich and Sarge came out of the sheriff's office to help with the processing of the prisoners. The three workers who had joined Collinsworth claimed ignorance of the deaths of any children. They were given the same choice as the ex-sheriff and were run out of the country. Those riding with Rodriguez all had prices on their heads. With too many under arrest to put them all in jail, Rodriguez's four men were locked in the local smoke house and a guard was posted outside. Rodriguez and Collinsworth were stuck in the same cell as Jammer, both of them cussing the Larkins for murdering children and getting them into this mess.

Things were under control and looking good until Molly arrived. She was disheveled, had tears in her eyes, and was out of breath from running. She rushed up to Dayton and grabbed hold of his arms.

'They took her!' she cried. After a couple of breaths, she added: 'A couple of men grabbed Alyson and rode off. I tried to stop them, but they knocked me down.'

Erich overheard her and moved to stand at Dayton's side. 'Wolfgang,' he stated angrily. 'It was Wolfgang.'

'You up for a ride?' Dayton asked him.

'I'll get the horses. You finish lining out things here.'

Dayton told Molly to go back and tend to the children. He expected news from many of their parents in the next day or two. Then he told Sarge what was going on. The man offered to help, but Dayton figured he and Erich could handle the job. Feeling a churning in his gut and terrible emptiness in his chest, Dayton's worst fear was that they would be too late!

11

Rico didn't like riding in total darkness. 'What's the hurry?' he asked. 'The gal is wanted for murder. No one is going to follow us.'

'Dayton Garrett will follow,' Wolfgang said, not advising him the warrant had been cancelled.

'He's only one man and he's busy with all of those gunmen.'

'I'm betting he's the one who broke Alyson out of jail — twice!' Wolfgang shrugged. 'I don't think he's going to quit chasing after her now.'

'We were hired by old man Bismark to bring the girl back alive. If we kill her, he might not pay the money he promised.'

'Things have changed.' Wolfgang was growing impatient. 'We do this my way now. I say we find a tree and string her up.'

'Do you have five hundred dollars?' Rico wanted to know. 'Are you going to pay us if your uncle makes a fuss over this?'

'I'll see you get paid . . . every dollar.'

Rico motioned to one of the Indians. 'We will do it tonight,' he said. 'But it's too dark out here to see your hand in front of your face.'

For himself, Wolfgang wanted to get this over with. But Rico was a man who actually enjoyed killing. He liked to take his time, terrorize his victim, torture them and watch them squirm in agony. When he finished he would look them in the face as the life left their eyes. He was a morbid, blood-lusting, sick-minded butcher, but Wolfgang needed him. He didn't want to face Dayton Garrett alone, and there was an outside chance he might catch up with them before they reached Shilo.

'What do you have in mind?' he asked.

'The Larkin spread will be clear of any workers,' Rico suggested. 'The kids were all moved into town and the men are in jail or running for their lives.'

'You want to go there?'

'Who would look for us at the main house? We take care of the girl, get a few hours' rest and pull out at first light. We can ride to Shilo, and you will fork over our money as soon as we hit town.'

Wolfgang knew Rico had a lot more experience than he did when it came to catching and killing people. He wouldn't risk being caught. Also, it made sense that everyone attached to the Larkin place would have abandoned it. Dead children had a way of raising people's ire.

'You're the professional,' he told Rico at last. 'We'll head for the plantation.'

★   ★   ★

Dayton and Erich were on the main trail to the fork where the road split. They assumed Wolfgang would ride towards Shilo, but otherwise had no idea where to look. The kidnappers could have taken Alyson to the nearest tree and left her hanging from a branch; they might be off the normal trail at a secluded spot, deciding how best to kill her at this very moment. They were floundering without a direction, yet they kept moving, because it was all they could do. It felt hopeless, the knowledge they could do little or nothing to change her fate.

'Someone on the trail ahead.' Erich cut into Dayton's nightmarish notions.

A shadowy figure, walking along the roadway, appeared before them. They drew closer and Dayton recognized the man from the Larkin plantation. It was Seeton.

*   *   *

Alyson mustered every bit of her bravado as she was pinched, grabbed and had her short hair pulled. The teasing would only be the beginning and Alyson vowed to give these animals as little satisfaction as possible.

'Look at her eyes!' Rico jeered. 'The hate is equal to her helplessness.'

'She's always been a haughty, proud little trollop,' Wolfgang said, feeling a surge of rage. 'Time she learned a lesson in how to be humble.'

'Let's bind her between the entrance-way columns, my friend. We will first take the fight out of her, before we have our fun.'

Wolfgang chortled wickedly. 'Right you are, Rico. We'll bust this uppity mare to ride.' He tore down a sunblind from a window and removed the cords. Each of them took one of Alyson's arms, snaked the cord around her wrist and secured the other end to the door frame. The distance was such that her hands did not touch either side and the bonds were so tight that they shut off the circulation in her hands.

Alyson strained against the bonds and set her teeth. An icy terror instilled a panic in her very soul, but she fought against it. Lacking any idea of rescue, she clung to the memory of being held in Dayton's arms. No matter what these men did to her, she would remain faithful, true to the man she loved.

The ripping of her dress brought forth a gasp. Within seconds she was stripped to only her lightweight chemise. Her body trembled and she cursed her weakness. Alyson knew she was going to suffer a worse torment than anything she had ever known before in her life. The quivering was reflexive and impossible to control.

'You see?' Rico laughed gleefully, recognizing her dreadful shudder. 'She is not so tough. She knows we will break her.'

'Wa'al, looky what I found!' Wolfgang said, picking up a riding quirt. 'Just what we need for the first lesson in obedience.'

'Try it out, my friend,' Rico encouraged. 'Let's see how much spirit this little filly has.'

* * *

Dayton and Erich had quietly approached the Yard House via the same route as Dayton had used when he visited Seeton previously. The slow-witted man had said one of the Indians was keeping watch, so they moved cautiously to the empty building.

After studying the place for a time they spotted the sentry. He was deep in the shadows of the main house, moving slowly, making a patrol around the grounds. That allowed them to slip in close enough to jump him and render him unconscious. As Erich began to tie the man up there came a woman's cry from inside the house, an involuntary scream of pain ripped from Alyson's throat.

Dayton whispered: 'I'm going in the back door. You take the front.'

Erich nodded that he understood as Dayton rushed to the rear of the house. Unfortunately, he had gone only a few steps when a body came hurtling through the air at him.

Dayton threw up his arms in time to

deflect the second Indian's savage strike with a wicked-looking knife. Ducking low, he went into a rolling block at the attacker's knees and upended him. Rather than do battle in the darkness, Dayton clawed his gun free and fired point blank into the man's chest. He knew it was a fatal shot. Springing to his feet, he rushed by the man's body and went through the back door.

He spotted Alyson, slumped against her bonds, her back showing a number of red welts, some of which had torn through the thin material of her chemise. It appeared she had passed out from the beating.

Alerted by the gunshot, Rico had backed into a corner and pulled his gun.

'Hold it!' Erich shouted, pointing his revolver at the man.

Dayton turned his own weapon on Wolfgang, but he leapt in behind Alyson. Using her as a shield, he produced a long hunting knife and put the blade up against her throat. It was a stand-off, with four men ready to kill or be killed. Erich held his gun steady, pointed at Rico, while Dayton had Wolfgang under his gun.

'This doesn't have to end with anyone getting killed,' Dayton said, aiming carefully.

'Kidnapping is a hanging offense,' Wolfgang sneered. 'Besides, this huffy little harlot killed my cousin, and my best friend. She's gonna die.'

Rico's eyes were alive and darting back and forth. He was like a cornered weasel, seeking an exit. There was a moment where no one breathed, not a sound could be heard, other than for each man listening to the thunder of his own heart. Then Wolfgang moved the blade slightly, as if he would begin cutting.

Dayton fired, putting a slug through Wolfgang's right elbow. The man cried out in pain as the knife flew from his fist.

Both Rico and Erich pulled their triggers — Rico only once, while Erich got off three shots.

Dayton swung about to try and cover both Rico and Wolfgang. Through the acrid smoke he saw Erich had his left hand tucked against his ribs. Rico had collapsed on to his face and showed no indication of having any life left in his body. Wolfgang backed up a couple steps and sat down on the floor. He cradled his damaged arm and began to wail from the pain. Dayton slowly holstered his gun.

'You OK?' he asked Erich, while moving over to help Alyson.

'Barely more than a scratch,' Erich replied. 'I saw Rico was going to pull the trigger so I didn't hesitate.'

'Good thing, or we might both be dead.'

'Thanks, Garrett,' Erich spoke sincerely, 'for not killing my cousin.'

'He won't be much of a bully any more,' Dayton returned. 'Tough to beat up on anyone with only one good arm.'

'You take care of the girl,' Erich told

him. 'I'll see about tending to his wound.'

The sound of gunfire had brought Alyson round. She managed to stand as Dayton used Wolfgang's knife to cut the cords from her wrists. With awareness returning, she frowned at him.

'What took you so long?' she murmured weakly. 'I thought you were my protector.'

Dayton grinned his relief and lifted her up into his arms. 'I was looking forward to the kisses and hugs I'd get for rescuing you. Guess that sounds a little selfish, huh?'

She didn't answer him with words, but turned her face upward so she could kiss him.

★   ★   ★

With the capture of Rodriguez and Collinsworth, Sheba and Walt told Dayton about the child slavery operation. They hoped to avoid the gallows by telling him everything they knew.

Dayton ordered a prison wagon and instructed Sarge about his duties. Then he turned to the final problem of finding and arresting the child slavers.

Alyson was not happy to have him go, especially with her being hardly able to move around because of the stiffness after the pain she had suffered. Also, little Debbie cried each time he started for the door of the boarding house. But this was something he had to finish. Alyson understood; she took Debbie in her arms and tried to make her understand too.

Dayton was saddling his horse when Erich arrived. 'I've got enough supplies for a week,' he offered. 'Think that will be enough?'

'You want to tag along with me?' Dayton was surprised. 'I thought you were taking Wolfgang back to Shilo.'

'He is going by stagecoach. The doctor bandaged my little scratch and fixed Wolfgang's arm in a sling. The big baby is drinking laudanum like it was cold beer. Hope he doesn't end up drugged out of his mind.'

'I'm glad to have the help, but the Anselmo brothers will not come along without a fight.'

Erich chuckled. 'I've learned that about you, Garrett — you're a very dangerous man to be around. I used to think your brother made up all the stories about you, but you are making a believer out of me.'

'The Larkins told me our slavers hang out at a trading post up near the Colorado border. It's a three- or four-day ride.'

'Paying Indians to steal children and then selling them into slavery is about the worst profession I can imagine.'

'If you're going to come with me, I'd better make you a deputy.'

'I've already got my sheriff's badge.'

'Yes, but becoming a deputy of a United States deputy marshal means you would actually have the authority to arrest this pair.'

'You're a US deputy marshal?' Erich was incredulous. 'And you broke a woman out of jail twice?'

'Justice sometimes takes the long way around to work,' Dayton said, not denying he was the culprit. 'Never had much luck working in a straight line. Take these child abductions. I had to start from this end, because I had no clue as to how to find out who was behind it from the other end. A small party of Indians grabbing a child here or there and no trace of what happened to them or where they went? Then, when a child of a friend of mine was taken, I began to search for missing children. Took months and months, but his name finally turned up as a ward of California. I never even thought about the children being taken a couple hundred miles and being sold into a form of slavery.'

'I'll never forget digging up those kids' bodies, Garrett. Swear me in and let's get started.'

★ ★ ★

Knute entered Ludwig's office and waited for the man to tell him why he had been summoned. Ludwig pushed a piece of paper across his desk.

'Wolfgang has a shattered right elbow,' he began. 'Courtesy of your brother.'

Knute picked up the telegraph message and read it.

'This says Wolfgang was bringing Alyson back here.' He scowled at Ludwig. 'She shouldn't have been going anywhere she didn't wish to go. You promised the charges had been dropped.'

Ludwig waved his hand in a helpless gesture. 'My nephew was being overly ambitious. I sent Erich to explain the situation but Wolfgang wouldn't listen. The bull-headed kid managed to get Rico and one of his Indian pals killed in his attempt for his personal vendetta.'

'Then you're not going to retaliate against Dee or Miss Walsh?'

'I wanted vengeance for my son's death,' Ludwig admitted. 'It was the hurt and pain of a grieving father, but I knew Alyson was innocent. Wolfgang won't be charged with kidnapping unless he ever goes near Alyson. Plus, he's going to be crippled for life. That ought to make him easier to manage. I suspect he will stop picking fights now that he probably can't whip anyone over the age of twelve . . . ' with a grunt, 'either boy or girl.'

'I'm glad things worked out.'

'Yes, well, I do have a complaint about your brother. You didn't tell me he was a deputy US marshal.'

'He didn't tell me either,' Knute replied. 'I thought he was looking for a missing child.'

'According to that telegram, he is taking Erich with him to Colorado to run down a couple of slavers. I don't like the idea of him requisitioning my son and risking his life.'

'This wire says Erich volunteered before he learned Dee was working for the marshal's office.'

'Do you trust him?' Ludwig asked

bluntly. 'I mean, can I trust him not to get Erich killed?'

Knute laughed without humor. 'The only thing I'm sure of about Dee is that he will get the job done. Usually he does it with the least amount of killing as is possible.'

Ludwig considered his words and sighed resignedly. 'All right, Knute. I guess we will both hold our breath until your brother's job is finished and Erich is back here safely.'

★   ★   ★

Three days had passed since Dayton and Erich left to find and arrest the child slavers. Alyson and Molly had been very busy and were glad to have Seeton working with them. All of the children liked him and he seemed as happy to be away from Sheba and the plantation as they were. Turned out Larkin had a sister, whose husband knew something of farming. They were taking over the Larkin estate and bringing in several farmers to share-crop the numerous fields. They would tend to the main houses and run the mill, while the share-croppers would set up camps or stay in the Yard House until they could put up permanent shelters.

The townsfolk voted to change the name of Larkinville back to Trespass, and had the signs posted before the prison wagon arrived to take away the prisoners. Their fate, after being tried for murder and assorted crimes, would be long prison sentences or hanging.

As for the kids, five or six got news daily about their families. The stage took a full load 'most every time it arrived. Now there were only the actual orphans left: eight unclaimed children between the ages of seven and twelve, for Molly to care for. Knute was handling the transfer of wards to her and also gained custody for Kenny, Ruby and Debbie, placing them into Dayton and Alyson's care.

Eager to have Dayton return, and worried about his safety, Alyson sat in the lounging room after the kids were in bed and simply watched through the only window. She knew it was silly to sit there pining away, as Dayton had said they would be gone for at least a week. Nonetheless, she spent her evening hours on the couch and often fell asleep.

This night Debbie came in and crawled on to her lap. She missed Dayton almost as much as Alyson did. Perhaps it was because they both owed him for their comfort and safety.

'You shouldn't be up,' she told the little girl without anger.

'Where do you think Daddy is?' Debbie asked.

Alyson smiled at how natural her calling him *Daddy* sounded. 'I don't know, dear. He's probably lying under the stars, staring at the night sky and wishing he was here with us.'

'Did your real daddy die?' she asked.

'He left when I was not much older than you. I don't know what happened to him.'

'Will my new daddy ever do that?'

Alyson put on a serious expression. 'Never.'

'But he is always trying to help people. How can he stay home if he's doing that?'

'We'll find a way for him to help people and still be home nights,' Alyson promised.

'Ruby said you are going to be our mother.'

'That's true, Debbie,' Alyson said. 'Dayton and I are going to adopt all three of you. We will all have a nice house and you kids will visit Molly's school to learn to read and write. We'll have a good life and a real family.'

'It all sounds like a dream,' Debbie murmured. 'A wonderful dream.'

Alyson felt the sting of tears. Debbie's words mirrored her own feelings. Then, discovering Debbie had gone to sleep, she offered up a prayer for God to please keep Dayton safe and bring him back to them.

12

Sometimes, just when a guy thinks he has caught a lucky break, he learns that luck had nothing to do with it — turns out the luck was deception. Such was the result of the trading post operator telling them where to find the Anselmos' camp.

The truth dawned on Dayton and Erich while they were still a half-mile from the slavers' supposed campsite. They were passing through a narrow gap between two hills when six Indians suddenly surrounded them, each with a fancy new Winchester rifle pointed at them.

Erich swore softly and raised his hands. 'Don't guess this was part of your plan?'

'Sonuvabuck!' Dayton exclaimed. 'We walked right into a trap.'

The ambush was so quick they had

no chance to react or fight. Both of them were disarmed, had their hands bound behind their backs, and were led to an Indian camp with four tepees and a large firepit. Another Indian, along with Hap and Cap Anselmo, came out to meet them.

'You've been dogging our trail for months,' Hap taunted Dayton. 'Collinsworth sent a telegraph message to the trading post and warned us that you were doing some snooping.'

'You won't be hearing from him again,' Dayton replied. 'He and the Larkins are in jail.'

'That's going to cost us a good deal of money,' Cap complained. 'With you nosing around, Tall Eagle and his boys had to stop grabbing kids until we got you off of our scent.'

'I don't suppose you two boys would like to surrender?' Dayton offered. 'It might just save your lives.'

Hap laughed. 'We know there are only two of you. And you are *our* prisoners.'

'Besides,' Cap added, 'kidnapping kids would get our necks stretched real quick.'

'You don't want to kill a deputy US marshal,' Erich warned them. 'The law will never stop looking for you.'

'Our problem,' Hap said. 'Your problem is about how long you want dying to take.'

Dayton directed his next words to the one Cap had called Tall Eagle. 'Must be some way to deal with this, chief, without any killing.'

The Indian gave his head a negative shake and scowled. 'Men must die.'

'All right, chief,' Dayton said gravely. 'If that's the way it has to be.'

'What are you saying?' Erich protested. 'Talk to them; make a deal.'

Dayton lowered his head. 'You heard what he said. Talking won't do any good.'

'Yeah, but . . . but . . . ' Erich couldn't find the words.

Tall Eagle issued a command in his native Cheyenne language. There was a short, yet seemingly endless, unbearable silence. Then six rifles erupted, spitting fire and lead and death. The echo of gunfire resounded against the nearby mountains, while smoke tendrils rose from each muzzle.

Erich nearly fainted, shocked to his boot heels. He stared agape at the bodies of the two slavers. Both Hap and Cap Anselmo lay dead on the ground. With his mouth still unhinged, he rotated about and stared at Dayton in disbelief.

'Guess that makes us even, chief,' Dayton said, regarding Tall Eagle with a sage expression.

'Even.' The chief repeated the word simply.

Two braves quickly cut the leather straps that had been around their wrists. Dayton and Erich took the reins of their horses and waited for Tall Eagle to speak.

'Ride away, man called Garrett,' the leader of the small band ordered.

Dayton didn't reply. He lifted his

hand in farewell and turned his horse around. Erich hurried to do the same and the two of them set off at a lope. They kept up the pace until they had covered nearly three miles. Then they slowed the horses to let them catch their wind.

'All right!' Erich shouted, unable to contain his questions further. 'You want to tell me what the hell that was all about?'

'Tall Eagle owed me a debt,' Dayton informed him. 'Now he doesn't.'

'You might have told me those Indians were part of your plan!'

'Actually, I didn't know Tall Eagle was a chief. I saved his life a few months back. When I saw he was in charge, I figured he would do the honorable thing. He ordered his men to kill the Anselmo brothers instead of us.' Dayton shrugged. 'Didn't really cost him anything. The brothers no longer had Larkin as a contact for ransoming kids, so their business arrangement was pretty much history. By killing them, the chief gets their guns, horses and everything else they owned.'

'They'd have gotten our guns and horses if they killed us too,' Erich pointed out.

'You're not complaining, are you?'

'Only about the five years of my life I lost when those guns went off. I'm about to become a father. I would sure hate to not be around to see my first child come into this world.'

'I guess we'd better get you back to Shilo, then.'

'What are you going to do?'

'I'll probably take over being sheriff in Larkinville — though I expect the name will be changed back to Trespass. Then I'll marry Alyson, adopt three of those kids and she can help Molly run her orphan home.'

'Good thing I sent in your claim for you.'

'Claim for what?'

'The bounty on Rodriguez and his men, plus Rico was also wanted in Utah. There will be a reward for him too. I reckon you'll get close to a thousand dollars altogether.'

Dayton was shocked. 'Well, now . . . half of that money ought to be yours.'

'My father is rich, Garrett. I'm already well off.' He grinned. 'You can use it to build yourself a nice home for your new family, and keep the rest until you are earning a decent living.'

'You might want to stick around for a day or so when we get back to Trespass. I'd be right proud to have you stand up with me at the wedding.'

'Best man?'

Dayton grined: 'One of the best I ever met.'

'I might consider it, providing I get to kiss the bride.'

'Molly has agreed to stand in for Alyson if there's any promiscuous kissing to be done.'

Erich laughed. 'Yeah. I'm sure that's the way my wife would want it too.'

Dayton was glad to have a plan for himself, Alyson, and their three kids. He said, 'Let's ride.'

'Don't worry about leaving me behind,' Erich replied. 'I'm with you all the way.'